Promise Me Forever

Promise Me Forever

RANDALL JAMES

Cover Concept:
Randall James

Cover Graphics:
Silke Stein

Cover Photograph:
Leslie Ann MacIsaac

Praise for
Promise Me Forever

"I'm absolutely loving the book. The characters make me feel as if I'm right there with them! I'm laughing out loud, love the surprises... and I don't want it to end!"

Leslie Ann MacIsaac, Cape Breton, Nova Scotia

"Every chapter captures my attention. Cannot wait for the next page. The writing brings us right into the story. Really enjoying it. Bravo!"

Priscille Belliveau, New Brunswick

"I love the story line and how all the local places and traditions are incorporated. It truly is a Cape Breton love story. I greatly enjoyed reading it."

Pearl Egdell, *Cape Breton, Nova Scotia*

"OMG, I loved it! The writing really got me into the book. I can't wait to read what happens with Logan and Rachel. 10/10. "

Susan Odo, *Cape Breton, Nova Scotia*

Author's Note

It is the first day of spring, and I'm so very excited to bring you *Promise Me Forever*. I'm really loving the characters and story development! We should be receiving the author's copy from the printer in a few days and, shortly after that, ordering the first books.

So, what was the inspiration for this romantic novella? If truth be told, for the first time ever, Silke and I watched a few Hallmark Christmas movies last winter. And in early January, this story idea popped into my head. Silke has been instrumental not only in editing, but giving me great feedback and offering her own ideas of where the story should go. The early readers also gave me tremendous feedback and encouragement to keep developing the story.

I love how both Rachel and Logan have grown in the story: *NY City Slicker meets Cape Breton Recluse*. But is she really a city slicker deep down? I hope you will love these characters as I do. (I'm already penning book two).

One early reader asked me if Logan was based on myself. I said 'no' at the time, but realized that he does have some things in common with my early life, as seen in my memoir, *Cape Breton Orphan*. In a way, I guess that all characters have bits and pieces of ourselves, and others that we meet throughout our lives — although these two are not directly based on any real persons.

So, please enjoy this story and let me know what you think. A rating or review on Amazon always helps. We have a Facebook group and website. You can see those links, plus acknowledgements and my book list, towards the back of the book.

Blessings!

Randall

March 20, 2024

Prologue

Promise Me Forever

Logan Stewart
CHAPTER 23

Connor was crushed. The icy fog gripped him, as he stood at the Low Point Lighthouse, gazing out over the grey ocean — the little he could see of it. How could he have been so wrong? How could he have misjudged things so badly?

Jessica was gone and his heart was shattered into a million pieces.

He couldn't sleep last night, or the two nights before that. Early this morning, he'd come to their favourite spot where they'd expressed their deep affection for one another. That had been only one week ago. He shook his head. After that moment, he knew they'd get engaged, get married — would spend the rest of their lives together.

His mind flew back over the summer. He'd taken her to every romantic spot: weekends at Bras d'Or Lake and Louisburg, picking blueberries in the hills of Low Point, walks along the seashore and trips to the lighthouse. She'd responded as he'd hoped. He now knew she loved him, as he her. His goal had been to get her away from Brett so that she could see it, and he had. It was the summer of bliss.

But two weeks ago, Brett had reappeared in her life and begged her to go back with him. She'd confided to Connor about Brett's texts, calls, and him showing up unexpectedly wherever she was. Connor had tried everything to block Brett, had tried every trick, but Brett was relentless in his pursuit of her. Connor wanted to confront his nemesis directly, but Jessica wouldn't allow it. It wasn't her way.

Brett was beating him again. Brett had been better than him at college sports and academics, and even in the business world. But this was a far different battle. Connor just couldn't lose Jess to Brett. He just couldn't. And deep down, Connor was convinced that this was just another conquest for Brett. He would take great delight in looking into Connor's eyes, once he'd won her.

So, Connor needed Jess to see it. To see Brett for who and what he was. The problem, was that Jessica was nice. Far too nice and naive. She wanted to let Brett down softly, and Brett knew it, using it to his advantage. He was devious. He was also a two-timing creep. Connor had been the one to inform Jessica about that after he'd spotted him dancing at a bar with his secretary. How cliche. But that was Brett. If a pretty girl wore a tight mini skirt, he couldn't help himself.

And yet, somehow, Jessica couldn't see it.

After Connor informed her, she finally confronted him. He had to admit it and then confessed to other affairs also. They weren't exactly affairs as they weren't actually married, but they were close to getting engaged one time, which is why Connor moved so fast. He knew that he was the best choice for Jessica and he planned on proving it. That was what this summer was all about. Connor could see her moving ever closer to himself with each passing day. Everything was working.

Then, a few days ago, she started to change. Her carefree spirit and laughter evaporated. She was in a constant state of thinking. What was bugging her so much? Deep down, Connor knew. Brett had gotten to her, and she was now deciding which man she wanted to spend the rest of her life with.

Connor had panicked a bit and pushed back on all the Brett stuff, which only caused a couple of arguments. There would be no forcing Jessica to make up her mind. Connor reminded her of the entire summer they'd spent together. She admitted she loved Connor, but what was unspoken in their arguments was that she cared for Brett also. That made Connor crazy. In his mind you could only love one person. *All* his fire, his flame, *everything* he had, was for Jessica. There was no one else and there never would be.

Recently, she was slow to answer his texts, and his calls went to her answering service. He felt the pit in his stomach. He had felt that before, when he'd been dumped years ago, in his early twenties. But he was now closing in on thirty. He couldn't lose Jessica. He just couldn't. But he had.

On Wednesday, she'd finally returned his last call, asking to meet at the lighthouse. He had shown up and she was already standing there. *Right here. In this exact spot.* He walked up to her and hugged her as they'd done a hundred times this summer. But he knew instantly that everything had changed. He stepped back and gazed into her eyes. At first she gazed back with a half smile, but then looked down.

He was devastated. He knew. She had somehow picked Brett.

"Connor, I have to talk to you."

"Save your words. You've chosen Brett."

Her eyes welled up.

"How could you? You know what he is. You know what he's done."

"He's says he's changed."

"Can a leopard change his spots?"

"We all make mistakes."

"Yes, but we grow and change. Not him. He's just tricking you."

"Connor ...."

"Look in your heart, Jess. Think of the summer we just had together. What more could I do to show you how much I love you. I know you love me."

She brushed a dark lock out of her eye. "I do love

you, Connor, but I have feelings for Brett also."

He was exasperated. "You can have *feelings* for a dog or a bunny rabbit."

She laughed. He loved making her laugh. They gazed at each other. She looked away and then turned back, locking her eyes on his. "I've agreed to go on a one-week cruise with him. He begged me for one final chance."

"*Manipulation*! He will act like a saint on that trip and then propose. Don't say I didn't warn you."

"I'm so sorry, Connor. We're flying out Friday night."

"That was fast."

She looked down.

"Yeah, don't worry about it. I'll be fine." That was a lie.

She stepped towards him and they embraced. He grasped the back of her coat. Was this the last time he'd ever hug her? He started to shake, and cried on her shoulder.

"Please, Connor, *don't*."

"What do you want me to do? You're my soul-mate. The one true love of my life."

She looked up, her eyes wet. "I have to go, Connor."

He wiped his eyes. "Yeah, I guess so."

She slowly walked away, looking back over her shoulder twice.

He just stood there, longing after her. A solitary, pathetic figure. Dejected. Rejected. It was a living nightmare. When she rounded the lighthouse and was out of sight, he broke down, sobbing.

A fog horn blared, instantly bringing him back to now. He realized his eyes were moist. Well, what was he to do? He could throw himself into the sea, but that never helped anyone. He gazed out over the ocean one final time and turned to leave. And there she stood. At first he thought he was dreaming or having a mental breakdown. She was a dark silhouette, slightly hidden in the mist, but it *was* her.

"*Jessica*?"

She moved towards him.

"Jess?"

"It's me. I'm back, if you'll have me."

"*If I'll have you*? This is unbelievable. Inconceivable. What happened?"

"Can I have a hug first?"

He embraced her. Hugging her so tight, she gasped. Holding her arms, he stepped back. "Is it really you?"

She threw her head back and laughed. Gazing at him, her eyes filled with tears. Tears of joy. Tears of love. Tears for him. *For him*!

She moved into him, lifting her head, her lips parting. He bent down. Their lips met. And so did their souls. He was in Heaven.

After a minute, they stepped back from each other again, still holding onto one another.

"All your warnings were in my head every moment

I was with him. I watched him like a hawk. And last night, when we boarded our flight for Miami, it happened."

"What?!"

"He had gotten us business class tickets. As we sat there and drank champagne, after having already downed a couple of drinks in the airport bar, he became chatty with the stewardess. He dropped his guard and struck up quite the conversation with her. It was like I wasn't even there. I even saw him checking out her legs while she waited on another passenger. He finally glanced at me, and realized I was staring at him. He made an awkward, funny face. Your words were echoing in my mind about him just manipulating me. I freaked out a bit, trying to quickly examine my options, and finally stood up and looked down the aisle. Passengers were still entering the aircraft in economy, so I told another stewardess that I felt sick and wanted to leave. Was it still possible? She said yes.

"Brett freaked out and shouted at me, demanding that I sit down. He was acting like a petulant child. They told him to calm down." She smiled. "Thankfully, it's still a free world. I grabbed my bag and exited. The airline even got my luggage off before the flight left. I took the next flight home."

"I'm so proud of you, Jess. You finally saw it. *Thank God.*"

She nodded, smiling. "I was so stupid for not

listening before, when you were desperately trying to tell me. He had some kind of hold on me, but it's over. Broken. I see him for what he is."

He gazed at her. "I almost threw myself into the ocean five minutes ago."

"I would have followed you."

"I might have drowned."

"I would've drowned with you."

"You would?"

"Yes."

He gazed deep into her eyes and knew it was true. He grabbed her and they kissed again. Long and deep. They stayed in each other's arms for what seemed like forever. He had won her heart. And that was all that mattered.

1

Cruising

Rachel Abrams fastened the top button of her coat, as the cool October wind nipped at her. Standing on the promenade deck, the view of Cape Breton was stunning. She'd heard marvellous things about this island in eastern Nova Scotia, and so far, her friends were not wrong. Red and gold leaves reflected early-morning sunlight through lush greenery and rolling hills. Houses dotted the countryside. She returned to her cabin, as the *Jewel of the Seas* docked beside the giant fiddle in Sydney.

The cruise ship would be in town for one day and Rachel would have lots of freedom to explore, but she still didn't quite know what she was going to do. Maybe she shouldn't have come by herself after all. She had offers from friends and colleagues to accompany her, but in the end, had decided that what she really needed was some time all to herself.

Scanning her small wardrobe, she went with navy

pants, a wine-red sweater and grabbed her fall coat. Stopping to look in the mirror, she examined her dark hair, which almost touched her shoulders. She really liked the shag she'd gotten before leaving New York. Her dark-blue eyes gazed back at her approvingly, as she studied her face. Maybe she was fooling herself, but she still couldn't see many wrinkles. *Not bad for forty.* She smiled. Once in a while, she could still turn a head. Satisfied with her look, she left the cabin.

A few minutes later, she walked off the ship. The first thing that caught her attention, besides the big fiddle and the Joan Harris Cruise Pavilion, were the rows of brightly coloured shops. She decided to start her adventure there as the little stores were already filling with fellow tourists. She browsed through a couple of them, which were selling t-shirts, mugs and many other gift items.

Rachel entered *Bree's Seaglass & More*, a small yellow shop sandwiched between a blue and red one. She noticed that they sold books and newspapers, besides sea glass jewellry and the usual trinkets. Stepping over to the sea glass displays, she admired some rings, pendants, and bracelets.

A brown-haired man in his mid-twenties, greeted her. She said 'hi' and kept browsing. Leaning against a bookshelf, she grabbed one book at a time and flipped through the pages. Most were written by an author named Logan Stewart. His genres were all over the place: science fiction, cozy mystery and even a romance novella. The blurbs were well-written and intriguing. And, even though the books were self-published, the covers were amazing. She collected two paperbacks, a hardcover, and a tshirt with a lobster on it, and proceeded towards the same smiling man who stood behind the cash register.

"How are you today?" he asked.

"Fine. How are you?"

He started to scan the items. "Great. Just visiting?"

"Yes, I'm on the *Jewel of the Seas.*"

"Nice. Where're you from?"

"New York." She noticed his intelligent hazel eyes.

He nodded. "Welcome to Cape Breton."

"Thank you." She pointed to the books. "A Cape Breton author?"

"Yes, and the romance novel is a local bestseller."

"Interesting. Have you read them?"

"Oh, yes. I read most of what my dad writes. I might be biased, but he pens great action scenes."

She chuckled and tapped her credit card. "I'm looking forward to reading them."

The man packed everything in a bag. "Great. I'm always interested to know what tourists think of Da's writing. He needs a bigger audience."

She smiled. "Thank you. Have a nice day."

"You too."

Rachel spent the rest of the day on the boardwalk and checking out the many shops of nearby Charlotte Street. Afterwards, she returned to her cabin. She felt exhausted from all that walking, so curled up in bed with the novels she'd purchased that morning. She started to read the cozy mystery, *The Library Affair*, which was surprisingly good, but soon fell asleep. Awaking an hour later, she walked out to her balcony and gazed down at the giant fiddle and couples strolling along the boardwalk. She sighed. It had never bothered her that much before, but she now longed for someone to enjoy the evening with. Turning the big 4-0 was starting to weigh on her.

Shivering, Rachel went back inside and picked up the mystery novel from off her bed. She smiled. Tonight, she was dining with Logan Stewart.

2

One Year Later

The cool autumn wind blew through her hair, as Rachel, once again, stood on the promenade deck of the *Jewel of the Seas*. Rounding the cape, the ship closed in on the port of Sydney. Low Point Lighthouse came into view. It stood on a piece of land that jutted out into the ocean, and had a unique red top. She smiled, recalling the last chapter of *Promise Me Forever*. The romance novella had moved her to tears. To think, that the final scene had happened right there. Connor had wanted to throw himself into that very sea. And there, Jessica had returned to him, appearing out of the fog. She sighed. *How romantic.* She made a mental note to visit the lighthouse if at all possible, and hurried back to her cabin.

A half hour later, and sporting a new red jacket, Rachel stuck her head into *Bree's Seaglass* and looked for the man who had waited on her last year. He wasn't present, but a young woman with baby-blue eyes and blonde hair was.

"Hi, can I help you?" she asked.

"Yes, I dropped in a year ago and bought a few books. There was a man behind the counter and we talked about the author."

"Oh, that's my husband, Mark. Let me get him." She headed towards the front of the shop and looked around the corner.

Two minutes later, the man, carrying a small box, entered. "Hi, can I help you?"

"Yes, I spoke with you last year about some books I purchased."

He set the box down and rubbed his chin.

She pulled out *Promise Me Forever* and held it up. "Your father is the author?"

"Oh, right!" He pointed at her. "New York?"

"Yes!"

"Back again, eh?"

"Yes, indeed, and mixing business with pleasure. Would it be possible to meet Mr. Stewart?"

"Business?"

"Yes, I'm an acquisitions editor for a large publishing house."

His eyebrows raised. "Wow. Da's a bit of a recluse these days, hiding in a local village called Low Point."

Rachel glanced at the author photo, realizing that the young man looked similar to his father. "Low Point?"

"Yeah — think green hills, blueberries, birch trees and a big lake."

"Sounds lovely."

"Yeah, it is, except when you get stuck there in the middle of winter under three feet of snow."

She chuckled. "Is it far?"

"About fifteen minutes away."

"So, it's not possible to meet?"

"Not these days. But ... well, to tell you the truth, I've been trying to get him out more." He grinned. "What do you think about an adventure?"

Rachel put the book in her purse. "I'm in."

"I'm Mark, by the way."

"Oh, right!" She stuck out her hand. "Rachel Abrams." They shook.

He raised his voice. "Bree!"

His wife appeared. "Yes?"

"This is Rachel Abrams from New York. I met her last year. She wants to meet Da and talk about his romance novel."

"Nice." She extended her hand. "I'm Bree." They shook.

"Nice to meet you."

Logan chopped down on another piece of wood, splitting it in two. Wiping sweat from his brow, he removed his blue-and-black checkered coat and threw it to the side. He grimaced — his back giving him pain — still not fully healed after all this time. He finished cutting the rest of the wood into kindling, gathered the pieces and brought them into the kitchen.

Walking back outside, he picked up his flannel coat and placed the axe inside the small red barn. He turned to his right and gazed at the hills. They'd sure gathered a lot of blueberries this summer. He smiled. Mark and Bree had come up on a few weekends and filled their buckets. Bree had then made blueberry muffins, scones, and pies — and had given Logan about half that she made. He loved that girl. Turning more to his right, he looked down White's Lane. The road disappeared into a sea of trees which reached almost to the shore, a half mile away. The dark-blue ocean was choppy on this windy October morning, the clouds moving fast across a blue sky.

Logan squinted as the sun peeked out between two clouds. He started to walk back to his small bungalow — white with blue trim — when he heard a car motoring up the road. He looked towards an opening in the trees and saw a red Toyota whiz past. He smiled. *Mark.* He waved as the car pulled up beside his blue Chevy truck. At first, he thought that Mark had brought Bree along, but now realized it was another woman.

"Hey, Da," greeted Mark, as the visitors exited the car and strolled up to him.

"Hey."

Mark gestured to the attractive woman. "This is Rachel Abrams from New York, in town with the *Jewel of the Seas.* This is my dad, Logan."

"Nice to meet you," they said in unison.

Mark scratched his forehead. "I met Rachel last

year, when she dropped by the shop and picked up a few books."

"Oh," said Logan.

The woman smiled. "Yes, sadly, I only read *Promise Me Forever* a month ago ... but I absolutely loved it."

"Thank you." Logan glanced at Mark knowing there had to be more.

She continued: "I wanted to meet you and—"

Logan sized her up quickly: *Striking. Chic. City Slicker.* "Would you like to come inside? I've got a pot of tea on and a couple of muffins waiting for me."

Rachel smiled. "Sure. Sorry if I interrupted your breakfast."

"It's no problem at all," assured Mark.

Logan opened the screen door and his guests walked through the pantry and into the tiny kitchen.

"Where, Da?"

"Let's sit in the living room."

"You guys sit down. I'll bring the tea," said Mark.

Rachel chose the rustic grey couch, while Logan sat in his black leather recliner.

"So, what brings you to Cape Breton?" Logan asked.

"My friends have been here a couple of times and they always rave about it, so I had to finally see it for myself. The first time was last year. I fell in love with the autumn leaves, the ocean, the fresh air, and, especially, the people." She sighed.

"Yeah, I lived in Calgary for a few years. I really liked it, but Cape Breton has that small-town feel."

She nodded, gazing out the window at the view he'd seen a few minutes ago. Her striking eyes matched the ocean; her makeup just highlighting her beautiful facial features.

"Here we go," announced Mark, entering the living room with a tray of tea and cups. He followed that up a minute later with a bowl of muffins and sat in an old brown chair across from Logan.

"Help yourself," said Logan, pouring the tea.

"Oh, *blueberry*," said Rachel, after munching on one. "Another reason I love this place."

"My fave," said Mark.

Logan noticed his visitor still wearing her jacket. "Would you like me to start a fire?"

"No, I'm fine, thank you — quite comfy."

Silence filled the air for a few minutes as they ate and drank. Logan saw Rachel looking around the room and wondered what she thought of his small house. He'd left in the original wood panelling, and put in a new wooden floor, covering it with an oval grey-and-blue rug. He refurbished the fireplace and bought a new coal stove and microwave for the kitchen. Power outages were getting too common in recent years, so he liked being mostly off-grid when it came to heat and cooking. His two-bedroom home had all that he needed.

Rachel turned back towards him. "Logan, as I was saying before, I thoroughly enjoyed your romance novella: the characters, setting, dialogue, descriptions

— everything. Well done. Is that the only romance book you have written?"

Logan glanced at Mark. "Yes, the first *and* last."

"Oh, I see."

"Yeah, my writing days are over."

"I'm sorry to hear that."

Mark sat his mug down and cleared his throat. "Da wrote this one two years ago. Everyone loved it and wanted a series, but ...."

"But, that was the end," interjected Logan.

Rachel nodded. "I see."

"Yeah, and, well, I'm kind of retired now."

Mark shook his head. "Da, you're only forty-six!"

Logan chuckled. "Forty-five, but who's counting. I injured my back working in the oil industry out west, and, well ...."

Rachel frowned. "Sorry to hear that, Logan .... So, no hope for a series?"

"Nope."

Rachel took a last sip of her tea and set the cup down. "I actually work for a large publishing house in Manhattan and we're looking for fresh voices."

Logan turned towards Mark for a second who was staring at him, his eyebrows raised — as if to say, *"Are you getting this, Da*?!"

Logan returned his gaze to Rachel. "I really appreciate the kind words and encouragement, but—"

"I understand, and I'm not one to push authors when they're dead set against a project."

Logan smiled. He didn't really believe that was true. She looked like a woman who didn't give up easily.

Mark jumped up. "Well, Da, we have to get going. I told Bree that we'd only be an hour, max."

Logan struggled to his feet, his back giving him some pain, as Rachel helped Mark collect dishes and bring them to the kitchen.

Outside, Logan hugged Mark as they said good-bye.

"It was great to meet you, Logan," said Rachel, waving and ducking into the car.

"Same here," replied Logan, as Mark jumped in, turned the car around and headed down the hill.

"I guess I wasn't much of a help," said Rachel, looking out the front window as they drove the highway towards Sydney.

"Yeah, you can see how stubborn he is." Mark gestured left and right. "This is South Bar, by the way. We live just up the road."

"Nice — a lot like Low Point. Why did he stop writing, I wonder?"

Mark frowned. "Well, his writer's block seems to have started when Carly, his girlfriend, left him two years ago. They moved here from Calgary, but she was originally from Victoria. She was a bit younger than Da and somewhat snobby, Bree and I thought. Capers are a different breed. They like to kid around, *a lot*, and can be mouthy and blunt, but they're also kind, honest and will give you the shirt off their back. Carly didn't really give them a chance, so, she didn't really fit in."

Mark pointed to his right. "That's our place, right there."

Rachel viewed a yellow single-storey house close to the ocean. A long driveway divided a large green yard, leading from the highway to the house.

"Wow, right on the ocean."

"Yeah, that's good on nice days but terrible in stormy weather. Bree doesn't like it when it gets too windy."

Rachel just nodded as she wanted Mark to continue with the main story.

"So, anyway, the whole thing with Carly really hurt Da, because we had all just moved down and he had this big fantasy of happily-ever-after built up in his mind. He loves this island and the people. Carly and Da started arguing all the time ... and then one day, he came home and found a note on the kitchen table. She was gone."

"Oh, that's terribly sad."

"Yeah. For all Carly's faults, he loved her a lot. Mark gestured again. "This is Whitney Pier. Famous back in the day for the steel plant. Towns like New Waterford, where Da grew up, and Glace Bay, mined the coal needed for steel making. The whole industry has been shut down since the early 2,000s."

"Interesting. I read some of that history in your dad's books."

A few minutes later, they arrived at the cruise ship

parking lot.

Rachel turned towards Mark and smiled. "Thanks for the great adventure and for introducing me to your dad."

"No problem. How long are you here for?"

"Two days, I believe. The ship has an engine problem that they're trying to fix, so I think we're getting an extra day in port. They're updating us soon."

"Would you like to have supper with Bree and me tonight?"

"Sure. I'd love to. What time?"

"Come to our shop about five."

"Okay, see you then." Rachel hopped out, waved and headed towards the big ship.

Once in her cabin, she flopped down on the bed, musing on the days events and reached for the small romance book. Flipping through the pages, she stopped at the author photo. She smiled. "Well, Mr. Stewart, let's see if we can't nudge you along." She closed her eyes and thought about the ruggedly handsome man who lived alone atop White's Lane, Low Point.

3

A Game of Hearts

S itting on the edge of her bed, Rachel stared at her shoe choices. She had no idea where they were going to take her. *Fall boots or high heels*? Both were black. She decided on boots to go with her black pants and magenta blouse. Grabbing her fall coat, she headed out the door.

Bree greeted her as she entered the shop. "So glad you're joining us tonight."

"I'm looking forward to it, but I forgot to ask if we're going to a restaurant or—"

"Nope! You're coming to our place."

"Wonderful."

Mark poked his head around some boxes in the back. "Hi, Rachel, be with you soon."

"No worries. I'm good.

A few minutes later, Rachel hopped into the back of their car, and not long after, they pulled off the main road and drove up the driveway to their house.

Walking to the front door, Rachel took a deep breath. "The air here is so fresh."

Mark nodded. "Yeah, I don't think I could move back to a big city after living here."

They entered the house and Bree took Rachel's coat.

Mark walked into the living room and gestured to the couch below the large window. "Would you like a drink?"

"Sure," answered Rachel.

Mark smiled. "Wine, beer or coffee?"

"If you two are having wine, I'll have a glass."

Mark nodded and headed to the kitchen.

Rachel sat down on the cushy dark-grey couch and looked around. To her left, and at ninety degrees to the couch, was a matching loveseat. A matching recliner sat opposite her. Paintings of prairie landscapes, and photos, hung on beige walls, and to her right was a fireplace with a beautiful mantel above it. Past the fireplace was a large entrance into the kitchen. The house was quite a contrast to Logan's in size and brightness.

"Mark's a beer guy," said Bree, settling down at the other end of the sofa, "but I'll be joining you in a glass of vino."

"Great!"

A few minutes later, Mark served wine to the ladies, and took a seat across from them in the recliner.

Bree and Rachel clinked glasses. "Do you like fish?" asked Bree.

"Oh, yes, love it!"

"Good, we're having smelts, a traditional Cape Breton meal."

Rachel thought for a moment. "Hmm, I don't know if I've ever had them."

"You're going to love them," said Mark.

Bree took a drink of wine and stood. "I'm going to throw them on now with potatoes and peas."

"Sounds sumptuous."

"By the way, I love your blouse," said Bree. "Very chic."

"Why, thank you."

"Must be lots of great stores in New York, eh?"

"Oh, yeah, Fifth Avenue has a zillion. Just ask my credit card."

Bree laughed. "Do you want to join me?"

"Sure."

The women strolled into the bright kitchen while Mark turned on the news.

Sitting on a stool at a small wooden counter, Rachel faced Bree's back as Bree whipped up supper at the stove. While they chatted away, Rachel swivelled on her chair and admired the kitchen. The top half of the walls were painted white; the bottom half were sea blue. A wooden table with four padded chairs sat below a window, and sliding glass doors led outside to a deck. The churning ocean seemed only a stone's throw away. She turned back towards Bree.

The kitchen filled with the wonderful aroma of the

small fish. Sipping more wine, Rachel thought that maybe she *had* eaten smelts, a long time ago. "It's possible I've had these before. Can't remember when, though."

"Ah, the smell is getting to you."

"Yes — yummy, yummy."

"More wine?"

"No, better wait for supper. I'm already feeling good."

They chuckled.

While they chatted away, Mark sauntered into the kitchen and set the table.

Rachel raised her voice so Bree could hear her above the cooking noises. "I love your kitchen colours."

Bree glanced at Rachel over her shoulder. "Thanks. Mark and I painted the kitchen and picked out the appliances together." She sighed. "I hope we can keep the house after all the time and money we spent." She turned for a moment to face Rachel. "The down payment took most of our savings, and the mortgage and taxes are so high. We had no idea things had gotten so expensive in Cape Breton."

Rachel frowned. "In the States too. I'm sorry to hear that, Bree."

Bree took another swig of wine and filled both their glasses. "Yeah, the move from Alberta was expensive enough. We were just starting to recover from that *and* Covid, when inflation hit. I just hope Mark doesn't have to go back out west for work." She turned back to the stove.

Mark cleared his throat. "Honey, I don't think Rachel wants to hear about our problems."

"Oops," said Bree.

"It's totally fine," assured Rachel.

A few minutes later, Bree turned and raised her hands. "It's all ready!"

Mark gestured towards a chair for Rachel. As Bree served the meal, the doorbell rang.

"Who could that be?" Mark asked, as Rachel and Bree took their seats across from each other. Mark threw the front door open. "Da! What are you doing here?"

His father smiled, stepped inside and closed the door. "Good to see you, too. Bree phoned and told me to drop by and pick up some smelts." Logan removed his boots and the men cut through the living room.

Sitting with her back to the wall, Rachel raised her eyebrows. The men walked into the kitchen, Logan wearing the same coat as earlier today.

Mark crossed his arms. "Bree, did you invite Da and forget to tell me?"

The night just got infinitely more interesting, thought Rachel, as she took another drink of wine.

Bree jumped up and hugged Logan. "Not exactly, Honey, but since he's here ...."

Logan and Rachel exchanged smiles.

Bree stepped back and looked at Logan. "Can you stay for supper?"

"I was just going to pick up the smelts, but if you've cooked enough ...."

Mark grabbed an extra plate. "We invited Rachel for supper."

Logan smiled again as Bree took his coat. "I can see that. We meet again Ms. Abrams."

"Indeed. Good to see you, Logan."

Once everyone was seated and served, Mark glanced at his father, who sat at the other end of the table. "Would you like to say thanks?"

He nodded and said a short prayer. Logan joined Mark in a beer, as everyone enjoyed the delicious fish amidst lively chatter.

Mark leaned over to Rachel, whispering: "Bree sometimes forgets to tell me things, like inviting Da over. Sorry."

Rachel grinned. "I can see that. She's wonderful. I love her personality."

"Me too."

Bree took another sip of her wine. "Well, Da, Rachel told me all about her exciting work as an acquisitions editor for Big Apple Books ...."

Logan stopped chewing.

Here it comes, thought Rachel, as a mischievous smile tugged at her lips. Go, Bree. Bree appeared slightly intoxicated, which added to her easy-going nature.

Bree continued, quite innocently: "Are you going to write some new stories?"

Mark coughed as Logan put his utensils down.

Rachel took a second to glance at everyone at the table. It was like an unfolding play.

Logan managed a smile. "Nope, that chapter of my life is closed."

"Well, I for one love your books," replied Bree, who stood up. "Would anyone like seconds?"

"The smelts are succulent," replied Rachel. "I'll have more, please."

Rachel tapped Logan's arm. "I have to agree with Bree. You're stories are so moving and emotional."

Logan gazed at her, his green eyes playful. "Thank you. And, I'm glad you don't push your authors when they turn you down."

Everyone chuckled in response to his answer.

"Another beer, Da?" asked Mark, hopping up from the table.

"Well, I should be going soon."

Rachel smiled. "Oh, please stay, Logan. The night is young and I promise to not mention your wonderful romance novel anymore."

"Yeah, c'mon Da, stay," agreed Bree, dishing out more smelts.

Logan rubbed his chin. "Well, that Canadian sure tasted good."

Bree and Rachel's eyes locked, as Bree picked up the wine bottle. "Would you like a top up?"

Rachel grinned and raised her glass.

After supper was finished and the table cleared,

Mark asked if anyone was up for a game of cards.

"The only card game I know is Hearts," answered Rachel, "and it's been ages."

"We love Hearts," said Bree, who grabbed a deck of cards off the top of the fridge, and handed them to Mark.

"Da always wins," said Mark, shuffling the cards.

"That's not true," said Logan, *"only most of the time."*

"Well, we'll see about that," answered Rachel.

Logan chuckled.

"Is this the game where you give away your heart?" asked Rachel, not so innocently, and glancing at Logan.

"Hearts," corrected Logan.

"Yes, that's what I meant," she responded.

"And watch out for the wicked Queen of Spades," added Mark.

"Yeah, I've had enough of those," joked Logan.

Everyone laughed.

Rachel studied Logan. It was good to know that he could laugh about such things.

"Can I get a coffee, please?" Logan asked.

"You bet," said Bree, who put a pot on.

For the next hour, they played a couple of games, with Logan winning the first game and Rachel winning the next one. After some more small talk, Logan looked at his watch. "Well, I should be going. It was a great night. Glad I stopped by for a minute."

Everyone laughed.

"Do you want some smelts to take home?" asked Bree.

Logan stood. "No, I've had enough for now. Thanks for the supper, Bree."

"You're welcome, Da. Anytime."

Mark got up. "Um, Da, would you be able to drive Rachel home? I think I've had one too many."

"Um, sure, it's up to Rachel." They all turned to her. She smiled. "I could get a taxi." *Why did I say that?*

"No," replied Bree. "You're our guest. We'll drive you home."

Rachel looked at Logan. "Okay, then."

They all walked to the front door.

"It's raining out," said Mark, looking out the window.

As Logan and Rachel put their coats on, Bree handed Rachel an umbrella. "Here, you might need this."

"Why, thank you, ma'am." Bree and Rachel hugged and everyone said good night.

Heading out, Rachel popped open the umbrella. It was cold and pouring. Logan unlocked the truck and opened the passenger door for her. He held out his hand to help her in. She took it and stepped onto the railing and into the truck.

"Thank you, kind sir."

Logan closed the door and dashed around to the other side. "It's raining cats and dogs," he said, as he buckled himself in.

Rachel threw her head back and laughed. "*Raining cats and dogs.* I love that saying. Who came up with that?"

Logan chuckled, turning the truck around. They waved to Mark and Bree who were waving out the living room window. Soon, they were on the highway. The rain and wind beat upon the vehicle.

Rachel glanced at the driver. "Well, that was enjoyable."

"Yeah, they're a great couple. Mark found a gem."

"Can I ask a question about writing, as long as I don't mention *the book*?"

"Sure."

"What made you start writing?"

He thought for a minute. "Well, when I was in high school, I loved reading. One time, a teacher read my book report out loud to the class. That was the first time that I thought that I could write. But after I graduated, I joined the Air Force and got posted out west — to Cold Lake, Alberta actually."

"*Cold Lake*?"

"Yeah. What a name, eh?"

She shook her head.

"True to its name, the winters were extremely frigid and we drank a lot. The next five years were a blur. I was just a young, stupid partier, who drank far too often. After that, I left the Canadian Forces and took a job as a labourer at a gas company. A couple of years after that, I got a job as an engineer's assistant at a large oil company. It was big money and crazy times, but six years ago, I fell off a ladder and injured my back."

"Ow."

"Yeah. And, well, long story short is, through all the medical treatments and rehab, I had lots of time on my hands, and I began to read again. I forgot how much I loved it. As I devoured books, I got a few story ideas of my own, which I wrote down in notebooks."

Rachel nodded. Maybe it was the wine, but the soft green glow of the dashboard instruments, the sound of the rain hitting the roof, the handsome man driving the truck, and the conversation on a subject she loved, gave the night an enchanting feel. *The dizzy, dancing way you feel.*

"And, that's when you wrote the romance novel?"

"I wrote that one about three years ago." The rain started to soften as they pulled up to the boardwalk. "Well, here we are."

She turned towards him. "Thanks for the drive home and for the lovely evening."

"Oh, you can thank Bree and Mark for that."

She smiled and gazed out the window. Although looking away, her thoughts were consumed by the man sitting next to her. He was so ... stable, friendly, and genuine. His thick, light-brown hair and dazzling eyes didn't hurt either.

"And what about you?" he asked.

She faced him. "What about me?"

"Well, how did you end up at a big publishing house? What attracted you to the literary world?"

She thought for a moment. "I always liked books. I read tons. I even wrote stories as a child growing up in Montana."

"*Montana?*"

"Yes, a small town outside Butte. Not too far south of Alberta. So, I know all about Big Sky Country. I grew up in the country. My dad had a few head of cattle and some milk cows, but later took a job at the post office. Mom was a part-time elementary school teacher. She raised my older sister and me." She smiled. "Some nights, we'd play a game. Mom or Dad would say a sentence and then each of us would add another sentence as we'd make up a wild story. It was such a great time. So, I've always loved storytelling."

He shook his head. "Wow, that's amazing."

"Yes, and even though I love my career and interaction with agents and authors, I spend far too much of my time dealing with the sales and marketing teams. I *hate* the bureaucracy side of the business. I *love* the creative side."

"I hear ya. I *love* writing, but I *hate* trying to find an agent or writing a detailed synopsis of each chapter of a new book. *Ugh.*"

"Yeah." She gazed at him. "Um ... you said *love.*"

"What?"

"You said *love writing.* Present tense."

He rubbed his chin. "Did I?"

She smiled. "Well, I should be going. It was nice to meet you, Logan Stewart."

"Likewise, Rachel Abrams."

He reached for his door handle, but she grabbed his arm.

"You stay right here. I'm sure I can reach ground safely." Rachel smiled, spun and opened her door. Climbing down, she waved and was gone.

Logan started the truck, but just sat there. He realized that he was attracted to her. It wasn't just her intelligent eyes and pretty face, but her hair, the way she moved — her gestures, her easy laugh. She waved again, and disappeared into the side of the ship. Logan shook his head. She was quite like a hurricane. He already missed her and hoped to see her again soon. But, wasn't she leaving in the morning?

4

Hide and Seek

After returning home, Logan called Mark. "What a great night. Thank you so much."

"Glad you had a good time, Da."

"I was wondering ... do you guys have Rachel's phone number and is she still in town tomorrow?"

"Let me check. Bree, do you have Rachel's number?"

"Nope. Sorry."

"She's still here tomorrow, right?"

"Yes, the ship has engine problems or something."

"Sorry, Da, we don't have her number, but she is here for an extra day. Did you have a good drive to the ship?"

"Yeah."

"Good, good. Going to ask her out?"

"Well, not on a date, but ...."

"You should, Da."

"Hmm. How will we get in contact with her tomorrow?"

"I'm sure she'll drop into the shop tomorrow morning. We'll call you."

"Okay, good night."

"Night, Da."

The next morning, a bright and calm one, Rachel appeared at *Bree's Seaglass & More* about ten thirty. Mark was busy with a customer, but Bree spotted her. "Good morning, Sunshine."

"Ha, ha. How are you today?"

"Bit of a headache, but otherwise, okay. You?"

"*Ugh.* Same."

"What are you up to today?"

"I'm not going out on any tourist trips. I'll just stay close to home, go for a walk and then visit some stores on Charlotte Street."

"Nice. I think Logan is trying to reach you."

That brightened her mood. "Really? Tell him to meet me on the boardwalk." She pulled out her sunglasses. "I'm going to need these, and a coffee. See you later."

"Bye!"

Logan's phone rang. It was Bree.

"Hi, Da. Rachel just dropped by. She's going for a walk on the boardwalk."

"Darn, I've got a load of coal coming, but the guy's late. Will be there as soon as I can."

"Okay — gotta run — tons of customers today."

Forty-five minutes later, Rachel popped back into the shop, which was still busy. She walked over to Bree, who was talking to a customer. As soon as there was an opening, Rachel said, "I'm heading to Charlotte Street."

As Bree rushed over to help at the till, she hollered back to Rachel: "I gave Logan your message."

Rachel waved. "Okay, bye."

A short time later, Logan pulled into the parking lot. He looked from the fiddle to the boardwalk, but couldn't see Rachel. He got out and walked on the boardwalk, heading left. He walked all the way down and back again, but saw no sign of her, so popped into *Bree's*.

Entering, he waved to Mark. "Have you seen Rachel? She wasn't on the boardwalk."

"Bree said she went to Charlotte Street. Sorry, Da, we're swamped. Hope you find her."

"Yeah, me too. Heading over there now."

Rachel enjoyed her late-morning stroll, window-shopping in a few stores. The one-way street reminded her of an old western town with two and three-story, wood and brick stores, only a few with awnings. It ran parallel to the boardwalk and was only a block away from the cruise ship terminal. Today, the street was bustling with tourists and locals. She stopped in a couple of gift stores, and later, browsed a ladies clothing shop. She tried on a couple of sweaters, but remembered that her suitcases were already jammed, so didn't purchase them in the end.

It was close to noon when she came across Daniel's Alehouse, a local pub. She stood outside and thought about going in, occasionally looking up the street to see if Logan might be coming. At that moment, a tall, dark-haired woman whom she had recently met on the ship, bumped into her.

"Hi, *Rachel*, right?"

"Yes, hi Jill."

"Isn't this a quaint little town?"

"Yes, love the Victorian houses."

"Me too, and the shops. I'm meeting my husband for lunch. Would you like to join us?"

Rachel tapped a finger on her chin. "Thanks for the invite, but I'm waiting for a friend." She looked up and down the street again.

"Well, I'm going to see if Ron already has a table. Hope to see you inside."

"Sounds good." Rachel waited another five minutes, then finally entered the pub.

Logan's back was aching as he walked down Charlotte Street, peeking into various stores to see if Rachel was shopping in any. He was starting to wonder if he should go back and get the truck. When he was just about to give up, he thought he saw her outside Daniel's, a couple of blocks down the road. As he squinted, the woman walked inside the pub.

He tried to hurry, but his back wouldn't allow it. A short time later, he entered the pub. His eyes adjusted to the light, as he strolled in. He looked around, spotting Rachel at a table, talking to a handsome, blond man who was drinking a beer. They were chatting and laughing.

Logan was stunned. He spun and walked out. *Well, that didn't take long.* Had he misread her last night? Maybe she'd just been overly friendly, or had too much to drink. Whatever the reason, it was a confirmation to him that he shouldn't give his heart away so quickly. What was he thinking? He'd been burned before. Twice. Fuming, he mumbled to himself all the way back to the parking lot.

Passing his truck, he stopped at the boardwalk, staring out at the water and sky. He shook his head and then headed for *Bree's*.

Bree spotted him. "Did you find her?"

"Yeah."

"What's wrong, you look like you just lost your puppy?"

"I should have known better."

"What?"

"I found her at Daniel's, having a drink with a man."

"Are you serious?"

"Yup."

"Da, listen to me. She popped in two times, hoping to see you. And don't you remember how she was last night? I think she likes you."

"Yeah, I thought so too, but maybe we just misread her friendliness. We don't actually know her."

"I'm sure there's a good explanation."

"Maybe, but I've been hurt too many times."

"Oh, Da."

"Yeah, plus my back is sore. I'm going home. Let Mark know."

"I will." A few customers entered and she had to break off the conversation. "I'll call you the moment I find out anything." She hugged him.

Logan limped back to his truck and drove home.

An hour later, Rachel dropped by the shop on her way to the ship. She felt exhausted.

Smiling, Bree walked up to her, while Mark manned the cash register. "Hi. Logan was here. He said he looked for you at the boardwalk and Charlotte Street."

"Really? How did I miss him. I looked everywhere for him."

"Yeah, and give me your phone number so I can reach you next time." They entered each other's numbers. Bree gently grabbed Rachel by the arm and escorted her around the corner. "He said he actually saw you at Daniels."

Rachel's eyebrows arched. "Huh? Why didn't he come in?"

"He did. He saw you sitting with a man."

Rachel thought for a moment and then laughed. "*He*

saw me with a man?"

"That's what he said. He was not happy and went home."

"That *man* is the husband of a woman I just met on the cruise. His wife was in the washroom."

Bree covered her mouth with her hand and tried not to laugh. "Oh, my goodness."

"Yeah. What is it with *men?*"

"Good question."

Rachel shook her head. "All he had to do was come over and say hi. We could have had lunch together. I can't believe it. I waited for him outside the pub for over five minutes, but couldn't see him, so finally accepted Jill's invitation to join them."

"Oh my goodness."

"Yeah. What am I going to do? I really like him, but this is ... well, crazy."

"Yup. A complete misunderstanding .... Do you have plans for supper?"

"No, just going to get some rest now, then pack up. We're going back to Boston tomorrow."

"Do you like pizza?"

"Oh, yeah."

"What kind?"

"Everything."

"Good. We'll get a couple. Meet back here at five?"

"Okay. Thanks for everything, Bree."

They hugged.

Bree looked her in the eye. "I'll fix this."

"Thanks. See you later."

Logan had just brought a bucket of coal into the pantry when his phone rang. He rinsed his hands quickly and grabbed it. "Hi, Bree."

"Hey, Da. Guess who just dropped in on her way back?"

"Rachel."

"Yup. I talked to her. Looks like you were right. She did indeed have lunch with a man."

"Ah."

"*And his wife*, who was in the bathroom. They are from the ship. She only met them a few days ago."

"Uh, oh."

"Yup."

He groaned. "I feel like such a fool."

"Yup."

"Does she know I know?"

"Maybe you should talk to her. I've got her number now, but I also invited her to pizza at five at our shop. Would you like to join us?"

"Yeah. That'd be great. I think I'll be having humble pie with mine."

She chuckled. "See you then."

"Thanks, Bree. You're the best."

Rachel strolled into *Bree's* a few minutes after five. Logan and Mark stood behind the counter and Bree sat on one of two chairs in the middle of the shop.

They all greeted her.

"Have a seat," said, Bree, as joyful as ever.

Rachel sat down and gazed at Logan, who looked a bit sad.

He cleared his throat. "I'm sorry I missed you earlier today. I want to explain what happened, after we eat."

She nodded. "Sounds good."

"What time are you leaving in the morning?" asked Mark.

"I think it's around eight. Will double check."

"Dive in," said Bree, grabbing a slice of pizza.

Rachel stood up and took a big piece. The women sat back down.

After everyone ate a couple of slices, Bree gazed at Rachel. "Mark and I had a long day. We're going to say good night now and we'll pop by in the morning to say good-bye."

Rachel frowned. "I'm kind of sad to be leaving. I feel like I've known you all for so long."

"Yeah, you're part of the family now," responded Bree. "You better stay in touch."

Rachel lifted up her phone. "Oh, I will." As the ladies stood and embraced, Bree whispered in her ear, "He feels bad."

Rachel nodded as they separated.

Mark rounded the counter and gave her a hug also. "What Bree said is true. You're part of our family now. We want to see you again. I mean after tomorrow morning."

She smiled. "Oh, I plan on returning. You can count on it."

She gazed at Logan, whose eyes were locked on hers. She knew they had to clear the air.

Bree hugged Logan, and they left, leaving Logan and Rachel alone.

Rachel sat back down and gestured to the chair. "Join me."

Limping, Logan walked over and sat down.

She faced him. "What happened to your leg?"

He smiled. "Oh, I walked too far this morning, looking for an old friend."

She smiled. "Did you find her?"

"No ... well, actually I did."

"Oh, good. Where was she?"

"She was sitting in a pub."

"Was she alone?"

"No, she was chatting with a man."

"Oh, interesting. Was it her boyfriend?"

"I don't think it was."

"Tell me more."

His face flushed. "Well, I have to tell you, Rachel, I actually thought you were having lunch with him. I felt jealous and left. That's the simple truth. I feel like a ... well, I feel like a fool."

"Good. Because you were a fool."

He shook his head and looked down.

She reached over and held his hand. "Logan, it's okay. We all make assumptions that we later regret."

He glanced at her through his bangs, which were getting quite long. For a moment, she was sidetracked by how good-looking he was.

"Yeah, I regret it," he said. "We could have had such a good day together."

"Yes. I was looking for you and waiting for you everywhere."

"You were?"

"Yes. I really like you, Logan."

"And I really like you."

"Then *trust* me. I'm not the kind of girl who plays games. Not those kind of games. I'm not the Queen of Spades."

He chuckled. "That makes me feel great. I've been hurt so often. I don't think I can take it again."

She smiled. "Let's finish our pizza and go for a walk."

He brightened. "That would be great."

After locking up the shop, they strolled along the boardwalk and chatted. The sun was just setting. It was a perfect night for a romantic walk, although a bit chilly. They passed other couples, some of whom greeted them. After walking for a while, they sat down on a bench. The darkening sky was mostly clear with a few clouds, a quarter moon shone across the water towards them.

Logan faced her. "So, you're off tomorrow."

"Yes."

"I'm going to miss you."

She smiled. "I'll miss you, too."

"Are you sure I didn't totally blow it today?"

"No, but we should take it slow."

"Yeah."

"You probably have some trust issues after your past relationships."

"Yup. I told you. I'm not good at this."

She chuckled. "Who is?"

They stared out at the water and moon for a while longer. It was peaceful. She knew it was the perfect time and place for a kiss, but the jealousy thing had put a slight damper on things. She had a feeling that Logan was the right one — the prince she had waited her whole life for — so she wanted to do it right. And she knew that Logan also needed time to process everything.

She yawned and stretched. "I can't believe how tired I am. I guess I'm getting old."

"*Older*," he said. "Definitely not old."

She stood up. "Walk me back?"

"Of course."

She shivered, as a gust of wind blew through her. "Man, it's getting cold."

"Yup. It's that time of year."

As they walked, Rachel felt something drop onto her shoulders — Logan placing his checkered jacket on her.

She smiled, feeling like a princess inside. "Thank you."

He stood there in only a black long-sleeve shirt.

"Aren't you cold?" she asked.

"A little. But I'm not freezing."

She shoved her hands and arms into the sleeves, and wrapped her arms around herself, snug in his coat. "This is *so* warm. No wonder you wear it all the time."

"Yeah, I love flannel."

She laughed and thought of her dad. "Men always have their favourite coats or sweaters, don't they?"

"Oh, yeah."

A she walked, she smelled something in the coat. Rachel smiled and hugged the coat again. It was more than outside odours, or wood or a fire. She smelled *him* too. It was a nice, manly smell. Not like the pretty boys in her world, who always smelled of cologne and after-shave.

At that moment, they arrived at the big fiddle. They stopped and faced each other.

She gazed into his eyes. "Thanks for the lovely walk. And, well, the whole visit."

"My pleasure."

"Oh, your coat." She started to unbutton it.

He put his hands up. "Please keep it."

"Are you sure?"

"Yes, of course."

"I'd love to have it. I'll wear it every time I'm cold. It will remind me of you."

"Yeah, the dumb lumberjack from Canada."

She threw her head back and laughed. "We don't all

think Canadians are like that."

They chuckled.

"I'm going to really miss you, Rachel."

"And I you." She gazed at him. "Don't give up on your writing, Logan. Don't let anyone ever take that away from you. It is your gift ... from God."

He smiled. "Thank you. That's sweet of you to say."

She suddenly felt that she'd been too hard on him. "Could we have a hug before I go? Even friends hug."

"Yeah." He hugged her.

His big arms surrounded her. He seemed like a bear. She squeezed him tight and looked up. Her eyes moist. "I should go."

"Alright. Please return."

"I will. I promise."

"I'm gonna hold you to that."

"Do."

She squeezed him again, then walked away slowly, looking back a couple of times. She wanted to run back to him, but knew it wasn't the right time. She hoped she wasn't making a huge mistake.

Early the next morning, she stood on her balcony as the ship left port, waving to her new friends. It felt like she was leaving family. It was astounding how fast you could get to know someone. These Capers were such a friendly people. Not just Logan, Bree and Mark, but many she met were like this.

Bree blew her a kiss at the end, which she returned,

laughing. She then locked her eyes on Logan's as best she could. Hers were moist. She wondered if his were. *Please bring me back soon.* They all continued to wave, until a few minutes later, when her friends were out of sight. She was now eager to see the Low Point Lighthouse on the way by.

As they cruised passed it, she thought about when she'd first arrived on this trip. She'd met the author just as she'd planned. And one day, she wanted to touch that lighthouse. She wanted to be there and gaze out at the sea and sky, just as Connor had done — just as Logan had done.

5

Back to Business

On Tuesday morning, Rachel entered her spacious office at Big Apple Books. Sitting on her desk was a beautiful bouquet of flowers in a turquoise vase. She hung up her coat, turned on the computer, and stepped to the window, overlooking the Hudson River. Cape Breton seemed like a distant dream. Had she really gone there?

A few minutes later, her assistant, Melanie, walked through her outer office and into Rachel's. "You're back!" she cried, stretching forth her arms for the hug.

Rachel realized how similar Mel was to Bree in height and appearance: both blondes and cheery — although Mel's hair was dyed and she often wore glasses. Circling around the desk, Rachel gave her a warm embrace. "Yes, I am, and ready to get back at it. And thank you for the lovely flowers."

Mel shook her head. "They're not from me."

Rachel's eyebrows arched. "Really, from whom

then?" She sat down in her black leather chair.

At that moment, Nick Hoffman sauntered into her office. "Welcome back, Rache! I missed you. How was your vacation?" Nick always looked like he just walked off the cover of a GQ magazine. His thick dark hair, chiselled features, tall frame and tailored Italian suits had many women swooning as soon as they met him. Rachel had been one of those women, five years ago, when Nick first joined the company as a top executive. The fact that he was the owner's son, made him even more attractive. Rachel was long over him, though.

She smiled. "It was a welcome diversion, but I'm glad to be back. We have a meeting at ten?"

"Yep — Marketing and Sales have questions about *Christmas in Manhattan*."

She rolled her eyes. "Oh, not that again. I thought everything was set."

"Well, we'll discuss it at ten." He turned to leave. "I hope you like your flowers." With that, he strolled out.

Rachel and Mel stared at each other, eyebrows raised. "*What the* ?" questioned Rachel, as Mel peeked down the hallway to make sure he was gone.

"Whoa!" said Mel, closing the door. "What was that?"

Rachel shook her head. "I have no idea. Has something changed since I was away?"

"Not that I'm aware of. Same old, same old." She lowered her voice. "I thought he spurned you years ago."

"Yeah, sort of." whispered Rachel. "It was mutual. And not only that, I met someone in Cape Breton."

"Really?"

"Yeah."

"Tell me *everything!*"

"I will, but not here. And I have the ten o'clock meeting that I have to focus on. Are you free to come over tomorrow night?"

Mel grinned. "Yeah!"

An hour later, Rachel strolled through sliding glass doors into the meeting room and sat in one of the white leather chairs. The cover of *Christmas in Manhattan* was displayed on a giant screen on the wall. Nick, who was also the editor-in-chief, sat at the far end of the long wooden table with fingers intertwined, watching department heads shuffle in and take their seats.

"Okay, let's get going," said Nick, glancing at his phone lying on the table.

Aiden from Sales held up a copy of *Christmas in Manhattan.* "I showed the new cover to my team and they still don't like it." Aiden looked like a librarian. He was middle-aged, mostly-bald and peered out at the world from behind oversized round glasses. He was put on planet Earth to oppose every book choice that Rachel ever brought forward.

Rachel tried hard not to roll her eyes. "What now?"

"It's too *Christmassey.*"

A chuckle escaped Rachel's throat. It was unprofessional. But thankfully, the design team and a few others others also chuckled and sighed.

"Too *Christmassey*? But it's a love story that takes place at *Christmas* in *Manhattan*."

"That's another thing," said Aiden. "We need a more subtle title."

"We don't have any more time for changes if we want to keep next year's schedule," replied Rachel.

"Can't you give in on this one, Aiden?" asked Nick.

Rachel did a double take, as Nick didn't normally come to her aid. Her nemesis made a half-smile. He didn't dare oppose the owners.

After dealing with a few other issues, Nick leaned forward. "Is there anything else for today?" He seemed distracted and in a rush.

Rachel held up her copy of Logan's novella. "I might have found a new voice in Cape Breton."

"What genre?" asked Lena from Publicity.

"Romance — *not* steamy."

"Interesting. Are you going to get us a copy?"

"Yes, I'll get Mel on it."

"It's already on the market?" asked Mr. Negative.

"Yes, but like most indie books, almost no one knows about it. We could scoop it. I'm in touch with the author."

"I want to read it," said Lena. Rachel could always count on her. Lena had been with the company about five years longer than Rachel. She was tall and thin with straight grey hair and, at times, kind of like the furniture — just always there. But at moments like this, Rachel realized how incredibly supportive she was.

Rachel mouthed *Thank you* to her.

"Me, too," chimed in a few others. The support from most of the other leaders made up for life with Aiden. Rachel was known for picking winners.

Nick knocked on the table. "Alright, get us ten copies right away. And Marketing, I want an update on all our big projects for this Holiday season, asap.

"Yes, sir," said Zach, as most stood up to leave.

Rachel and Nick stayed behind after everyone else had left.

"Thank you for the flowers, Nick." She tried to sound genuine.

He smiled. "You're welcome. Like I said, I missed you."

"That's sweet. But *flowers*? It will start rumours."

"Let them talk." His phone pinged. "Got to run. Mother wants an update."

Later in the afternoon, Nick dropped by her office, again. "Are you free on Friday night? I've got something important to discuss with you."

She felt uncomfortable. "Hmm."

"We'll go to *Frenchette*, your favourite restaurant."

Manipulation. "I don't know, Nick."

"I have a big decision to make for the company. I need your feedback. In fact, it concerns you."

"*Me*? How?"

"Friday night?"

"Alright." Thinking of Logan, she felt a bit guilty.

Standing at the living room window of her third-floor condo, Rachel looked out over her Stamford, Connecticut neighbourhood. The sun was just going down. She shook her head. Recently, another condo building had gone up close to her. The whole city was changing, and way too fast. It was already a growing financial centre, starting to rival Manhattan, and the population was growing leaps and bounds each year.

Still, she loved the city and Connecticut, especially her favourite spots, like West Beach and Cove Island Park. And she loved the scenery — the autumn leaves changing colour, and the distinct four seasons running into each other. She loved the whole feel of New England. In many ways it was similar to Cape Breton.

Maybe it was just turning forty this year, but on the way back from Cape Breton she'd done a lot of thinking. Thinking about Logan and his family. Thinking about Cape Breton. Thinking about Montana — her mom, dad and sister. And, now, Nick suddenly interested in her again after all these years? She couldn't put her finger on it, exactly, but she had the feeling that change was in the air.

The doorbell rang, jolting Rachel from her musings. She saw her reflection in the window and chuckled. She was still in her blue pyjamas and absolutely didn't care. It was that kind of day. She just wanted to be comfy.

"Come on in, Mel," she said, opening the door and hugging her friend.

"All dressed up for me?" Mel asked, sporting black leggings and a green sweater.

"Ha, ha. I think I still have cruise lag."

They entered the bright living room, where Mel flopped down on the dark-blue sectional.

"Are these new?" Mel asked, pointing to abstract prints that hung on the wall above the sectional.

The set of three reminded Rachel of large rocks — some turquoise and some black, on white backgrounds. "Nope. They were here last time you visited."

"Hmm. I love them."

"Me, too. The set has a cheery feeling." Rachel sat on the arm rest of a white chair. "Is this a wine or coffee night?"

"Coffee. It was a long commute. Work comes early."

"Smart girl." Rachel went to the kitchen, turned the pot on and returned, dimming the lights and settling in at the other end of the sofa.

Hugging a pillow, Mel grinned. "So, tell me everything. How was Cape Breton and *whom* did you meet?"

"Cape Breton was lovely. A picturesque island and salt-of-the-earth people. Their thick maritime accents are wonderful. Low population. Feels like living in the country."

"Nice. *And*?"

"*And* ... last year I picked up a few books from a local author, and this time I got to meet him. Logan Stewart. That was the order I gave you today."

She nodded. "What does he look like?"

Rachel grinned. "Aren't you interested in his writing?"

"We'll get there. What does he look like?"

"Handsome. One or two inches over six feet. Incredible green eyes. He's kind of quiet. Doesn't talk a lot."

"Wow."

"Yeah. And I met and spent time with his son, Mark, and Mark's wife, Bree. She's a riot. Reminds me of you. Let me grab the coffee." She returned with their mugs full and sat back down.

"Does he only write romance?"

"He writes various genres, but what caught my attention was the romantic novella. It was so moving and set in Cape Breton. I think our readers would really like it. We'd have to spruce it up a bit and get him to expand the story or make it a series. But, therein lies the problem."

Mel took a sip of her coffee. "What?"

"He stopped writing a couple of years ago after a breakup."

"Oh."

"Yeah, but I think I can nudge him along."

Mel grinned. "If anyone can, it's you. That's your forte."

"Thanks. I just have to be sensitive. I think he's warming up to me a little."

"Oooo."

"Yeah, we had a fabulous meal of smelts at Mark and Bree's place and Logan happened to drop by." She laughed. "Bree and I drank too much wine, but it turned out good as Logan had to drive me back to the ship in the pouring rain. We had a wonderful chat. He's such a nice guy. Strong. Reliable. I felt like I had known him longer. Easy to talk to."

Mel raised her eyebrows. "Uh, oh."

"What?"

Mel leaned forward, hugging her pillow. "I think you're *falling in love*."

Rachel laughed. "Maybe."

"Mixing business and pleasure?"

Rachel took a sip of her coffee. "Yeah, hmm."

"And, what was that with Nick and the flowers?"

"Crazy. He dropped by later and invited me out for supper on Friday night."

"What?"

"Yeah, he said he has a big decision to make for the company and it involves me."

Mel put her cup down on the coffee table and gazed at Rachel. "Be careful, my friend. I just don't trust him. He seems to be moving fast."

"Yeah, I feel it too. There's something afoot that he's not revealing."

"I guess you'll find out Friday night."

"Yeah."

"Call me right after."

"I will."

On Friday evening, Nick sent a limo that drove Rachel to Frenchette. She strolled in and mentioned a reservation under Nicholas Hoffman. While she waited, she looked around. The soft lighting, and cozy booth area, created a relaxing and romantic atmosphere at her favourite restaurant.

Appearing a minute later, the manager brought her to a booth. "Would you like a drink while you wait?"

She sat on the inside cushy seating, leaving the chair on the outside for Nick. "Yes, a bottle of Chardonnay please." A minute later, a young waiter poured her a glass and left the bottle.

A few minutes after that, her phone pinged.

Nick: Sorry! Will be there in ten.

She was famished and not impressed with Nick, so decided to order a steak and fries immediately. Frenchette's had the best in town. While she waited, she spent the time on her phone looking at photos of Logan, Bree and Mark. The meal arrived before Nick, so she went ahead.

The waiter stopped by. "How is everything?"

"Excellent. Thank you."

He smiled and left.

Just then, Nick rushed to the table and sat down. "I'm so sorry. Had a meeting with Mother. He poured himself a glass of wine."

The young waiter stopped by."Would you like to order, sir?

"Yes, I'll have what she's having. Sirloin steak — well done. "

The waiter nodded and left.

Rachel took a drink. "What's the big news?"

"You're looking at the new owner of Big Apple."

"What?"

"Yeah, Mom and Dad are stepping back and they want me to take full control." He raised his eyebrows and stared at her, expecting some incredible response.

She couldn't muster much, and still didn't understand how this would affect *her*. He was already, in many ways, the de facto owner at most meetings anyway.

She faked a big smile. "Congratulations, Nick."

"Thank you." He took a big swig of wine. "You're probably wondering how this affects you."

"Yes."

"Remember years ago, when we dated a few times?"

"Of course."

"Well, I wasn't ready to settle down. I was immature. But I've grown a lot, and ..."

"Yes?"

"Don't you see?"

"See what?"

"This is not just *my* future we're discussing, but it could be *our* future."

She put her utensils down and sat back. "Um, Nick."

All she had thought about during her first week back in town was Logan. And, although they were roughly the same age, Nick and Logan couldn't be any more different. Logan was a man. A caring, tender, strong man. And Nick. Well, Nick was a boy in a man's body. And, although, sometimes that could be fun, Rachel was looking to the future and her plans, and Nick was not fitting, at all.

Nick leaned forward. "All I'm saying, is that I want us to start dating again." He tried to hold her hand, but she withdrew it.

Rachel leaned forward as her eyebrows knit together. "This is *not* a date, Nick." She pointed with her index finger to him and herself. "*This*, right here. *Not* a date."

He shook his head, as if stunned. "Well—

"No, we are two friends having dinner and discussing business. That's what I agreed to."

Nick took another big gulp of wine and looked for the waiter. He finally spotted him. "Hey, what's taking so long!"

"Sorry, sir, let me check."

Nick shook his head. "The service here is really going down."

Rachel shook her head. "You just ordered, Nick." She'd never seen him so agitated. She was starting to wonder if he was on something.

A short time later, the waiter reappeared with Nick's meal. "Here you go, sir. Sorry for the delay." The flustered waiter was obviously new. "Can I top up your wine, sir?"

"Bring another bottle," Nick said, as he cut into his steak. "Buffoons! It's *medium rare*." He threw down his utensils. "Take this away and get me the manager."

"Yes, sir." The scared waiter almost fumbled the plate taking it away.

A minute later, the manager appeared. "Yes, sir."

"The waiter is an idiot and the cook made me the wrong steak. I ordered *well done*."

"I am very sorry, sir. There must be a mix-up. We've had the same cook for five years. He is excellent. The waiter is in training. I will speak at him,"

"Perhaps he should find new employment."

"Nick!" Rachel whispered loudly.

The manager's face reddened. "Perhaps *monsieur* could be patient. We will correct the mistake and the meal is on us." He nodded and left.

Rachel assumed Nick's anger was a response to her resistance. Did he really think she would agree to date him so quickly?

Nick gazed at her and smiled. A weak recovery attempt. "Sorry. Where were we? Oh, yes. You used to have a dream about owning your own publishing company, correct?"

That caught her off guard. "Yes."

"Do you still dream of it"

"Yes."

He cleared his throat. "Well, don't you see?"

"That's quite a leap, Nick. Is this a meeting or a

marriage proposal?"

He grinned.

Her face flushed. "I wasn't expecting this, Nick. This is way too much, way too soon. I think I'm going home."

"*What*? *Why*? I haven't even gotten my steak yet."

"Well, I ate mine alone." She grabbed her purse, rose and put on her coat.

"At least let me drive you home."

"No, I'll grab a cab. Good night, Nick."

At the front door, Rachel tried to pay for her meal, but the manager wouldn't allow it. She pulled out a twenty from her purse. "Please give this to the waiter. I thought he was wonderful."

The manager smiled and took the bill. "Thank you, madame, I will tell him."

That night at Frenchette's seemed to have cooled Nick's heels, as he didn't ask her out again. For the next few weeks, Rachel put her head down and worked hard. And each day she thought about Logan, Bree and Mark. She toyed with the idea of surprising them for Thanksgiving — American Thanksgiving — but decided that would be too forward at this point.

Normally, Mel would pop over and they'd go shopping on the Saturday of the long weekend, but some of Mel's family had unexpectedly arrived in Rochelle, so she had to cancel. Rachel would just hang out in Stamford and visit her favourite places, alone.

At least it would be peaceful and she could think about her future.

On Saturday evening, during Thanksgiving weekend, Rachel's phone rang. Joy flooded her heart, as she stared at the number. "Hi, Bree!"

"Hey, Beautiful, how's everything in the big city?"

Rachel laughed. "Busy, busy. I actually live in Stamford, Connecticut and commute every day to work."

"Nice. Wow. Got time for FaceTime?"

"Oh, that'd be great. Let me fire up the laptop. A few minutes later, there they were, face-to-face. "It's so great to see your smiling face, Bree."

"Likewise. Happy Thanksgiving, by the way."

"Thanks! You already had yours."

"Yup, eon's ago, in October. And all the turkey you can eat for a week afterwards."

"Ha, ha."

"Eek! Your coat!"

Rachel looked down and realized she was wearing Logan's jacket over her pyjamas. "Oh, yeah. I forgot. It's so comfy."

Bree grinned. "We're all here, by the way."

Rachel's face flushed and she felt butterflies. Bree moved aside and Mark and Logan appeared, waving.

"Hey, Rachel," said Mark.

"Hey, Mark."

"Hi, Rachel," said Logan.

"Hi, Logan."

Bree's head popped back in front of her. "We all want to know when you're coming back!"

"I actually thought about surprising you this weekend, but decided against it."

"You should have come!"

Rachel frowned. "Yeah, probably. I could kick myself for not calling you and planning it."

"How about you come for Christmas?"

"Really?"

"Yes!" chimed in Logan and Mark.

Logan pressed in beside Bree. "Come back soon. We miss you."

She had to resist the urge to kiss her screen. "And I miss you. All of you."

"Nice jacket," said Logan.

Hugging herself, Rachel nodded, gazing at his stubbly face, wishing so much she was there with him, with them. "Yeah, I love it. I wear it on cool evenings. Reminds me of a big lumberjack I know in Canada."

They all chuckled.

Bree sat in the middle again, with the men in the background over each shoulder. "Then it's settled — you're coming for sure!"

"Yes, just message me the date you want me to arrive."

"I will asap."

"By the way," Rachel said, "they owe me tons of vacation days, so I *could* come early."

"*Really*? How early?"

"Fifteenth? Twentieth?"

"Oh, goody. I'll message you later today."

"Great!"

"Okay, talk soon."

They all said good-bye and the Facetime ended. Rachel jumped up and studied the kitchen calendar, flipping to December.

6

Christmas

Strolling through the arrivals entrance of the Sydney airport, Rachel spotted Bree, who ran up to her and gave her a tight hug. "How was your flight?"

"Perfectly fine. I still can't believe they let me use the company jet. I'm so glad to be back!"

"Here, let me take a suitcase. The car is not far." They walked out and within a few minutes were on their way to South Bar. It was one week to Christmas and scattered flurries blew through the air. And, although it was only four in the afternoon, it was already getting dark.

Bree glanced at Rachel. "Mark's picking out a tree, as we speak. We wanted to wait until you were here to decorate it together."

"That's so sweet of you guys."

Bree cleared her throat. "By the way, are you Jewish? Mark mentioned to me last night that you might be. We thought we'd check to make sure you celebrate

Christmas. Sorry, for not asking sooner."

"No worries. Yes, I celebrate Christmas and Hanukkah. I'd say I'm mostly secular, though. Hanukkah falls during Christmas this year."

"Really?"

"Yes. My father was Jewish, but Mom was a strong Presbyterian. The two holidays at the same time were never a problem for them. Growing up in Montana, we celebrated mainly Christmas, but Mom made sure there was always a menorah for Dad. That was the only thing he asked for, besides Christmas. I can still remember him lighting a candle each night and saying a little prayer. As far as Christmas, he was all in."

"That's so sweet."

"Yes, it was." She smiled. "Two things always happened in our house with Mom. No matter who you were, you got a full plate of food and you heard about Jesus. My parents brought home more than one straggler over the years."

Bree chuckled. "She reminds me of my grandfather. He lives in a small town outside Calgary. He's the same way."

"Sweet."

"Your parents are passed away?"

"Yeah, Dad passed away suddenly ten years ago, and Mom early last year. My older sister took care of her."

"I'm sorry."

"Thanks."

"Are you in contact with your sister?"

"No, not really. We became estranged over the years."

"Ah, that's too bad."

"Yeah. She didn't think I supported her that well when my mom got sick and passed away. And then she had to handle the selling of the home and property. I was super busy at that time, and couldn't get out there as much as she wanted me to, so ... yeah."

Bree reached over and squeezed her hand. "Sorry."

"Thanks. She also has her hands full with three children and four grandchildren."

"Wow."

"Yeah."

Bree turned off the highway. "Here we are."

"Wow, look at that!" Standing in the yard, which was blanketed with six inches of snow, was a massive snowman, a penguin, and a few giant candy canes, all of them lit up. Christmas lights ran along the roof edge and circled the white posts just outside the front door."

Bree shut off the car. "We left the outside lights on just for you."

Rachel squeezed her hand. "Thank you, Bree."

Grabbing the suitcases, they entered the house. "Let's leave them in the entrance," said Bree, hanging up their coats. "We have your room all prepared whenever you want or need some private time. How about a cup of coffee?"

"I'd love a cup. Thanks."

They strolled into the kitchen, where Bree turned on the coffee pot. "I love your outfit. So chic."

"Thanks!" Rachel wore a navy-blue business jacket with matching pants, and a white turtleneck. "And I love your blouse."

"Yes, magenta. Inspired by a friend of mine."

Rachel laughed. "I think I wore something similar last time I was here."

"Yes, you did. Now, tell me all about New York. What have you been doing the past couple of months?"

Unbuttoning her jacket, Rachel sat down at the table. "Mostly arguing with Sales and Marketing and pushing my favourite authors and books, including Logan's. I'm so looking forward to this downtime."

"By the way, something I wanted to ask you before ... have you ever had any serious relationships in New York?"

"Ha, ha. You remind me of Melanie, my friend in New York. When it comes to romance, she wants *all* the details. As long as it's about me."

Bree grinned. "Well?"

"There's not much to tell. I did have some dates over the years, but none of them really developed into anything serious."

Bree set mugs, cream and sugar on the table. "Come on. You're a pretty, dynamic, acquisitions editor of a major firm. Surely you've had some suitors over the years."

"Um, not really. As you can tell, I'm married to my

career."

Bree poured the coffee and sat down. "Hmm."

Rachel gazed at her. "Well, there was one man who showed some serious interest, but it's a long story and I'm trying to figure him out."

"*Oh, goody.* Tell me about him."

"Okay, but don't say anything to Logan, just yet. His name is Nick, the owner's son. He's tall, handsome, dark hair and eyes, and, when he first joined Big Apple, about five years ago, I had a *huge* crush on him. A few years ago, we dated a couple of times, but nothing came of it."

"Wow."

"Yeah, he's a playboy, and I realized that he was not the one for me."

"Hmm."

"Yeah, but the interesting thing is, when I returned from Cape Breton, he bought me flowers and supported me in team meetings and dropped by my office to chat. He then invited me out to dinner to tell me he was taking over as the sole owner."

"Uh-oh."

"Yeah. So first, I informed him that our dinner meeting was not a date, and secondly, that I wasn't interested in him. Between you and me, my heart is somewhere else."

Bree took a sip. "And, that's great to hear."

"Yeah. Well, the sudden interest was quite tempting, because my dream is to own my own publishing company one day."

Bree smiled. "Really?"

Rachel nodded. "Yes, but I want a boutique publishing firm. I want to really connect with authors and agents, and perhaps, bring out only three or four titles a year. Find the gems. Have a small team of maybe four or five people who love books and stories as I do."

"Sounds great."

"Yeah."

Bree took another drink of coffee and set her cup down. "If you opened a business here, we could all help. Logan is an author, I took journalism for two years, and Mark is great at marketing."

Rachel grinned. "You're full of surprises, Bree. I didn't know you took journalism."

Just then the doorbell rang a few times. "Mark!" exclaimed Bree. Rachel followed her to the door, where they threw the luggage in the closet. Bree opened the door and there stood her husband with the tree. It was a fair size with a dusting of snow still on the branches.

"What do you think?" he asked, as he shook it off on the door step.

"Love it!" said Bree.

"Me, too!" chimed in Rachel.

"Oh, hi, Rachel, great to see you again."

"Same here."

Bree grabbed the top of the tree and they carried it in together — Mark throwing off his boots on the way.

There was a spot already cleared in the corner beside the couch, where Mark set it in the stand as Bree held it straight. Once it was secure, they all backed off and admired it.

"It's perfect, said Rachel.

"Okay, let's have some more coffee," said Bree, as they all moved into the kitchen and took their familiar seats.

"Is Logan coming tonight?" asked Rachel, her voice a bit high. She hoped she didn't sound as excited as she felt.

Mark gazed at her. "Yup, should be here soon."

Rachel felt her face redden, as a wonderful sensation rippled through her heart. They would be together again any moment. She felt as giddy as a schoolgirl.

Ten minutes later, the doorbell rang and the door opened.

Mark walked into the living room and greeted his father who removed his boots. "Hey, Da."

"Hey."

Bree and Rachel were right behind Mark.

Logan faced Rachel, his eyes sparkling from the light of the fire. His smile was wide and warm. "Hi, Rachel. Great to see you again."

Rachel extended her hand, trying to control her fluttering heart. "So nice to see you again, Logan. How have you been?"

"Same old, same old." He handed his parka to Mark, revealing a purple sweater.

Bree embraced him. "Da!"

"What would you like to drink, Da?" asked Mark on his way to the kitchen.

"How about a beer?"

"How about an eggnog?"

"A special one?"

"Yup."

"Okay, but only one."

Mark grinned. "You got it."

Bree faced Rachel. "I'm going to open a bottle of Chardonnay. Will you join me?"

"My favourite. How did you know?"

"I didn't," replied Bree, smiling.

"I swear you two are sisters," said Logan.

Being likened to young and beautiful Bree made Rachel feel great. Rachel sat at one end of the couch and Logan settled into the far end. Bree soon handed her a glass of wine and left again.

Mark returned, handed his dad the drink and turned the radio on. *White Christmas* was playing and Rachel suddenly felt in the Christmas spirit. Manhattan, work and Nick seemed a million miles away. She was in the same room as Logan, and that was all that mattered. Bree and Mark being two of her favourite peeps, didn't hurt either.

A short time later, Mark threw another log on the fire. Bree carried in a box of decorations and placed it on the carpet. A minute later, Mark went to the basement and returned with a box of Christmas lights.

Mark and Bree checked out the lights and hung them on the tree. Bree then knelt down beside the box of decorations. "Come and help me, Rachel."

Rachel came over and knelt down as Bree started removing ornaments from the box. Bree selected a couple and started to hang them. "Grab whatever strikes your fancy," she said to Rachel, who soon stood beside her picking out spots on the tree that needed to be filled.

Mark went back downstairs and returned with another box. He opened it and dropped a handful of tinsel into Logan's lap. "Once the girls are done, we get to throw tinsel on the tree."

"Nice," said Logan, gathering it.

At that moment, the news came on the radio. At the end of the local news segment, the weather lady announced a coming snowstorm.

"Sounds like we're going to get some snow in a couple of days, said Logan.

"Maybe it won't be so bad," replied Bree, who seemed unconcerned.

Rachel noticed Logan and Mark exchanging looks, though.

A short time later, Bree and Mark brought in platters loaded with Christmas treats: fruit cake, various Christmas cookies, nuts and chocolates.

"Would anyone like some coffee or tea?" Bree asked.

"Tea for me, please," replied Logan.

"I'll have some tea, too," said Rachel.

"Coffee for me, Hon," said Mark.

A short time later, Bree served the drinks.

The radio station resumed playing holiday tunes and belted out Boney M's Christmas medley. Rachel had flashbacks of her childhood, decorating the tree and house with her family. She felt warm and cozy inside. She hadn't felt like this in many years. Even when she shopped in New York at Christmas for her co-workers and friends, she felt lonely. The City had over eight million inhabitants, and yet it was filled with lonely people just like her.

As they decorated and sang along with the radio, she caught lots of looks from Logan. Each time, they smiled at each other. They were like teens with crushes. She really wanted some alone time with him. A short time later, the tree and living room were completely decorated.

The fire crackled. "Anyone interested in supper?" asked Bree, getting up.

"I'm stuffed," replied Rachel. "Plus, I ate shortly before I took the flight."

"None for me," replied Logan.

"I can snack later," answered Mark.

"Well, that makes it easy," said Bree.

An hour later, Logan announced that he was leaving.

"We've got a big day planned tomorrow, said Mark, sitting in his recliner and looking at Rachel.

"Really? What are we going to do?"

Logan stood, walked over to the entrance and put

his boots on. "It's a surprise. You'll see tomorrow."

Rachel smiled. "Oh, good. I love surprises."

Bree handed Logan his parka and embraced him. Rachel wished it was her hugging the big guy.

"Good night," he said to everyone.

"Drive safely," Rachel replied.

"I will," answered Logan, opening the door and heading out. They all waved to him from the window.

Bree turned to Rachel. "Come, let me show you your room."

Mark grabbed Rachel's suitcases and rolled them to her door. Her bedroom was right across from theirs. Bree and Rachel brought the suitcases into the room, as Rachel looked around. It was a small room with a queen-sized bed covered with a blue-and-white quilt, two night stands with lamps, a dresser with a mirror and a closet. Bree walked over to the window and opened the curtains. Rachel soon stood beside her and smiled. The partially hidden moon shone off the water. She couldn't believe she was so close to the ocean. "I love this view," she said.

"Me too," answered Bree.

Rachel yawned.

"I think you're ready for bed," said Bree, who also yawned.

"Oh, yeah." They embraced. "Thanks for everything, Bree. I really mean it."

"Anytime," Bree said, as she left and closed the door. "Good night."

"Good night."

Rachel put on her pyjamas and climbed into the sack. As she lay there, she mused about the day's events. She thought about decorating the tree and the fun night. She really felt like a member of the family. She studied the quilt. It had wonderful winter scenes in each section, including snowmen. She pulled it up around her shoulders and snuggled into it. Soon, she was off to dreamland.

7

Winter Wonderland

Rachel awoke to the smell of pancakes and coffee. *Yes!* She hopped out of bed, pushed on her slippers and headed down the hallway.

"Good morning!" sang Bree and Mark.

"Morning," returned Rachel, taking her usual seat at the table beside Mark.

"How did you sleep?" asked Bree, cooking at the stove.

"Wonderful. That quilt was so warm and lovely."

"It was my grandmother's."

"Wow. Thank you."

Bree served blueberry pancakes and smiled at Rachel. "For today's adventure, we're going skating at Petrie's Lake, which is right behind Da's house. Do you own a pair of skates?"

"I do, but they're in Connecticut." She ate a few bites of her pancakes. "These are sumptuous. I love blueberries!"

Bree grinned. "We know."

"Let's go to Mayflower Mall first and pick up a pair of skates," suggested Mark.

"Sounds, great," replied Rachel, "but I'm not that great of a skater. I only go once in a blue moon."

"That's okay, said Bree," sitting down across from her.

"Have you ever played hockey?" Mark asked.

"A couple of times in Montana, when I was a kid."

"What way do you shoot?"

"I have no idea."

"Well, Bree shoots left, so we'll get you a right handed stick, just so we have both."

She grinned. "You expect me to skate *and* play hockey?"

Mark chuckled. "We can teach you to play pretty quickly."

"Don't worry, said Bree, "I'll be with you the whole time. It'll be a blast."

Two hours later, Rachel, sat in the back of the car with her new white skates in a box. She felt butterflies as they turned up White's Lane. Was her excitement for skating or for seeing Logan again? It was both, she decided. As they made the final turn at the top of the road, she saw Logan standing outside with his stick and skates. A foot of snow covered the ground.

The visitors exited the car with all their gear and walked up to Logan. Rachel shivered, as the icy wind cut through her parka.

"How's everyone this morning?" asked Logan.

"A little bit of a headache, but otherwise fine," answered Bree.

"Good," said Mark and Rachel.

"Great! Follow me," said Logan.

They trudged along, following a path beside the barn and headed towards the lake through the trees.

"I haven't skated in two years," said Rachel, who was right behind the leader.

"Oh, don't worry, we're not pros," said Logan over his shoulder.

"*Sure*," said Rachel, not really believe that.

A few minutes later, they stepped onto the lake. It was massive and surrounded by trees. There were already other people skating at different sections along the edges, far away. Rachel's group sat down on a big log and laced up their skates. All wore toques and gloves. A few minutes later, Logan stood, skated around a little and then stopped in front of Rachel. He held out his hand. She looked up, smiled, took his hand and rose.

"The skates fit well," she said, as she took a few strides. She could see everyone's breath, including her own, as they spoke.

"Hey, you're a pretty good skater!" exclaimed Bree, already striding around. Soon they were all skating, laughing and enjoying themselves. Rachel felt increasingly confident the more she skated.

A few minutes later, Mark grabbed two sticks,

skated over and handed Rachel one. "Try this," he said. "I'm right handed. So you hold it like this with your right hand on the lower part."

She held it just like Mark showed her. For a second she had a flashback to her youth, playing hockey on Miller's Pond with her sister and their friends. She grinned. "Yeah, this feels right. This is how I gripped my stick as a kid."

Bree and Logan grabbed their sticks and skated over. "You look like a natural," said Bree.

"Thanks. We'll see."

Logan produced a puck from his pocket and threw it down on the ice. He smiled. "This is a soft-rubber puck. So, it won't hurt you if you get accidentally hit."

"Thanks." She was actually worried about getting hit with it, so that eased her fear. As she gazed at him for a second, she realized how thoughtful he was in everything.

Mark scooped the puck with his stick and zipped across the ice.

Bree took off in another direction, tapping her stick on the ice. Mark fired a pass to her. She took the pass, turned around and shot it towards Logan, who looked at Rachel. She took the hint and skated away.

She turned around and waited for the pass, trying to balance herself with the stick on the ice. Logan shot it to her. She was a bit slow and awkward with the stick, so the puck flew well past her and stopped about thirty feet away, towards the centre of the lake. As she skated after it, she noticed how dark it was below the surface. That was actually the water under her. *Crack.* At that moment, a loud noise travelled from right under her skates across the lake. She shrieked and turned back to Logan — terrified.

Seeing the fear on her face, he raced over. Reaching her, he put an arm around her back. "It's just the ice cracking," he said.

She wrapped her arm around him and held him tight.

He squeezed her. "Don't worry."

She looked up at him.

He gazed down. "Are you okay?"

She nodded.

"Alright, stay here, I'll get the puck." He skated off and returned. "Let's play closer to shore." They skated in, and for the rest of the time, played towards the edge of the lake. Rachel knew right then that this was the man she wanted to spend the rest of her life with. Her fear had vanished and her joy and comfort had returned.

Although they were having a blast, the icy wind was nasty and after a further half hour of skating and hockey, they skated over to the log, where Rachel noticed their boots were getting nice and cold.

Mark faced his father. "Da, you were skating great out there."

"Thanks. It's been a while."

Mark gestured to his own back. "But, *your back.*"

Logan's mouth fell open. "You're right! I didn't even think about it out there." Father and son fist-bumped.

Rachel was ecstatic to hear that.

"I'm freezing!" said Bree. "Let's go for some hot chocolate."

I love that girl! Rachel was so happy Bree spoke up. Rachel and her frozen fingers wanted to leave, but she didn't want to appear wimpy in front of these hardy Canadians. "Great idea," Rachel replied.

Ten minutes later, Logan threw his gear in the pantry and joined them at the Toyota. He jumped in the passenger seat as the foursome drove off to New Waterford. Mark pointed out various sites along the way, as they drove through Low Point, New Victoria, and finally, entered New Waterford. Rachel enjoyed the warmth of the car as much as the conversation.

As they drove through New Victoria, Bree pointed left, down a road. "The Low Point Lighthouse is right down there."

"Maybe we can stop on the way back?" suggested Mark.

Logan looked out his window to the right. "Maybe."

Bree leaned over to Rachel with gritted teeth and eyebrows raised, making a funny face. Rachel knew what she meant. Logan, obviously, still had emotions that surrounded the lighthouse.

After driving around New Waterford for ten minutes, and looking at various places, like where Logan grew up close to shore, and where he went to high school up by Scotchtown, they made a pit stop at Mickey D's, a popular local restaurant, where each of them grabbed a hot chocolate — Logan paying.

A few minutes later, they huddled in the warm car, chatting, and then Mark drove off, heading back towards New Victoria. As they closed in on Browns Road, Mark asked, "Da?"

"Sure," Logan replied, and Mark turned right. They drove up to the lighthouse, and parked close by. Rachel loved the big red hat that sat on the seventy foot structure. The lighthouse stood on a section of snow-covered land that pushed out into the ocean.

"Let's go!" said Bree, and they all got out and walked towards the tall building. Rachel made sure to touch it; another item crossed off her bucket list.

Carrying their cups, they walked around the lighthouse a couple of times and then stood together on the side facing the rough sea. Even though it was freezing and windy, Rachel appreciated the isolation and beauty of the lighthouse and area. No wonder Logan had picked this spot for the grand finale. It was so romantic. She wondered how often he and Carly had come here. She glanced at him. He peered out towards the horizon, perhaps remembering those exact things. Rachel was proud of him for making this step today.

Bree and Mark strolled around the lighthouse, leaving her and Logan alone.

"It's a lovely spot," said Rachel. "I remember seeing the lighthouse on the way in on my last cruise."

Logan turned towards her. "Yeah, it's nice."

She sipped her chocolate that was cooling rapidly. "Thanks for taking me skating today. I had a blast."

He smiled. "You did great."

"You don't think I'm a wimp?"

He chuckled. "No. I was terrified the first time I heard the ice cracking. Still freaks me out sometimes." He stood closer to her, sipping his drink.

She didn't know if she should go there, but took a chance. "So this is the famous lighthouse."

He glanced up at the red topper. "Yup. First time I've been here in ages."

"It was a lovely scene."

He gazed at her. "Yes, but it was inspired by my love at the time. Carly. I couldn't deal with it after she left me."

"Bree told me a tiny bit about it."

He nodded. "It's hard for me to get past it. Like I said, I'm not good at this love thing."

She stepped closer and gazed deep into his eyes. "Maybe you just never met the right person."

He returned her intense gaze with a smile. "Maybe you're right."

She leaned into him, touching his arm.

He held her arms and lowered his head.

Her lips parted.

"Can we go, it's freezing!" shouted Bree, rounding the lighthouse.

Logan stepped back quickly.

"Oh," said Bree, smiling. "I'm sorry."

Rachel chuckled. "It's okay."

Marching around the lighthouse, Mark saw everyone looking at each other. He smiled. "Did I miss something?"

They all laughed.

Later that afternoon, the foursome sat at the kitchen table playing a game of Hearts. As Rachel played her cards, she once again felt like she was part of the family. The chats, the activities, growing closer to Bree, Mark and Logan. She felt so comfortable with them. She was amazed that she hadn't had these thoughts in ages.

Her mind wandered.

She loved her job and had never wanted to have children, but was rapidly changing her mind about that now. She smiled. *I'm way too old to have a baby.* She chuckled inside herself as she thought about being pregnant. She glanced at Logan and smiled.

He returned her smile.

If you only knew what I was thinking, Logan. As she played her last card of that round, her phone vibrated. She picked it up to see who was calling. *Nick*?! *Great.* She decided to answer it. "I think I better take this. Hi, Nick."

"Hey, Rachel. Guess where I am?"

"Where?"

"Cape Breton."

Rachel was stunned. "*What*? What are you talking about?" She felt all eyes on her.

"I'm in Sydney, at the Holiday Inn. I need to talk to you."

"Are you serious?"

"Yes, Mother sent me. There's some big changes happening this week. Also, she has a big offer for you. I need a quick answer."

Rachel flushed. "I'll call you right back."

8

Surprises

Shaking her head, Rachel laid the phone on the table. "That was *Nick* — my boss and the owner's son. He flew in on their private jet and is at the hotel in Sydney." She rolled her eyes. "I can't believe this."

Bree locked eyes with her, knowing this was bad news for Logan. "He's *here*?"

Rachel nodded. "Yup." She faced Logan. "I have to go. I need to settle this right now."

"What's it about?" asked Mark.

"It's complicated. The owner's are stepping away from the firm and want Nick to take over and they want to make some kind of offer to me."

"Well, that sounds good," said Logan.

Rachel bit her lip. "He's also interested in me."

Logan frowned. "Oh."

"Yeah, I dated him a few years ago, but it didn't go anywhere. Lately, he's been pursuing me, but I have warded him off, till now."

101

"Why did he have to fly in? Why didn't he just call?" asked Mark.

"Good questions," answered Rachel, who was starting to feel like this was all her fault. She should not have borrowed the company jet. Nick was using that favour as a way to get close to her again.

"Yeah, I don't like it," said Bree. "Do you want me, or any of us, to go with you?"

"No, I feel like I have to address this myself."

Logan gazed at her. "Can I drive you?"

"Yes, that'd be great. Thank you."

A short time later, Rachel and Logan stood at the front door. Bree hugged her tight. "Don't let Nick, or anyone, bully you into anything."

"I won't."

After saying their good-byes, Logan and Rachel climbed into the truck. Soon, they were on the highway. A few minutes passed without any words being spoken.

Logan glanced at her. "Is there any possibility that you are flying back to New York with him?"

She looked out her side window. "I doubt it, but he said there was some big offer from Vanessa, his mother."

"Sounds like she's the driving force."

She turned back to him. "Yes, very perceptive."

"Be careful, like Bree said. Looks like pressure tactics."

"I will be careful."

They closed in on the hotel. "Logan, I really enjoy your company."

"Me, too."

She laughed.

He glanced over. "I mean with you."

"I know."

He smiled. "I hope you can stay. I will greatly miss you, if you go back."

"You will?"

"Yes, of course."

"Why didn't you call me in all this time?"

"I thought you wanted me to take it slow."

"Yeah, but I didn't mean *that* slow. We only had the one FaceTime. I was hoping that you'd call me yourself."

He shook his head. "I almost called you a thousand times."

She sighed. "Why didn't you? Men are so stupid."

"Yeah, sometimes we are."

He pulled up to the hotel entrance, shut the truck off and faced her. "My feelings for you have only grown."

She gazed deep into his eyes. "I never stopped thinking about you since I met you. I just wanted to make sure that you're the one."

He laughed. "I can't believe it. You're a big city slicker and I'm a grubby, injured oilfield worker. You have such feelings for me?"

She smiled "Remember, I'm a country girl at heart."

"I know."

He pointed backwards with his thumb. "Why don't we turn around right now and go back to Mark's?"

"I'd love to, but I have to address this now."

"Should I wait?"

"No, go back. I will call you or Bree as soon as I can."

"Are you sure?"

"Yes."

Logan hopped out and rounded the truck. Opening the door, he held out his hand. She took it and stepped down.

He smiled. "One last thing before you go in."

"Yes?"

"I started writing again."

She grabbed him, hugging him tight! "Are you serious?!"

He wrapped his arms around her. "Yes, I think you'll like book two in the series."

She stepped back and gazed into his eyes. "Logan, I'm so proud of you!"

"Well, it was you who pushed me and inspired me." He grinned. "Can you recommend a good agent?"

She raised her eyebrows and pointed her finger at him. "You don't need an agent. I'm taking it whether Big Apple does or not." She stood on her tippy-toes and kissed him on the cheek. "I'll see you soon."

He held her. "Do you promise?"

She gazed at him with all the truth and sincerity in her, knowing how important the question was. "Yes."

She then hurried off towards the entrance, looking back to wave.

As she entered the lobby, she turned her attention to Nick — fuming.

Logan touched his cheek where she'd kissed him and climbed back into the truck. He fought the urge to follow her in and protect her from Nick. But, as much as he hated to, he had to be an adult and go back to Mark's and wait — the hardest thing for him to do.

Nick was waiting for her in the lobby. "What is it Nick, and how dare you follow me to Cape Breton? Are you a mad stalker now?"

Nick raised his hands in protest. "Whoa, whoa, whoa. Would I have flown here if it wasn't uber important. Mother wants to talk to you."

Rachel was stunned. "Vanessa is here?"

He pointed to the elevator. "Let's talk in my room." They took the elevator up and soon stood in his executive suite. He gestured to the couch where she took a seat, and walked over to a dresser. He grabbed his phone and appeared to text someone. He then pulled out the top drawer of the dresser and turned back to her. "How is your vacation going anyway? How's the local author?"

She pursed her lips. "I could say it's none of your business."

Nick abruptly knelt down and presented her with a

small red box.

She was taken aback. "Nick, what are you doing?"

"Well, I won't see you for Christmas. This is an early present. He placed it in her hand. "Open it."

"Nick, I can't."

"Why not? We've known each other for five years. We dated. I arranged the flight to Cape Breton for you."

Staring at the box in her hand and going against her better judgment, she opened it. A huge diamond stood elegantly on an gold band. Of course, the diamond sparkled like crazy. "*Nick.*"

He smiled. His eyes hopeful. "Before you say anything, I've thought a lot about this moment and about our relationship. There's no one else I can envision leading the company with and spending the rest of my life together with. Will you marry me?"

All she could see in her mind was Logan's warm green eyes gazing at her. How he comforted her on the ice. He almost kissed her at the lighthouse. She knew she loved him. At the same time, visions of a mansion, big cars and being co-owner of Big Apple danced in her head. She was a tiny bit weak-kneed. Her eyes locked on Nick, who was turning red, waiting for her answer. "Nick, the ring is lovely, and I *did* care about you in this way, a long time ago, but ..."

His eyebrows knit together. "You do realize the offer in front of you? We would be owners together. Imagine walking into the boardroom and dealing with

Aiden as the owner."

She chuckled, trying to diffuse the moment. She should have listened to Bree and Logan and not come. "Yeah, it is tempting ..."

He abruptly stood. "So, what's your answer?"

He had turned back into the petulant child that she'd witnessed at Frenchette's. She handed the box back. "I'm sorry, Nick."

Grabbing the box, he shoved it into his jacket pocket. He marched over to the dresser and picked up his phone, texting again.

What is he doing, now? Rachel fought the urge to storm out.

A moment later, Nick's phone rang. He took the call and put it on video. "Hi, yes, she's right here." He walked over and handed Rachel the phone.

Shocked, Rachel stood up. She was suddenly face to face with Vanessa Hoffman. The owner was in her mid-seventies with silver hair and grey-blue eyes — which were staring at her under angled eyebrows. She wore a bright red top, long gold ear rings and a scowl.

"Good afternoon, Rachel." Her voice was deep.

"Good afternoon, Vanessa."

"I was hoping this would be a celebratory call — Nicholas having bought you a fabulous engagement ring and having flown all the way to Nova Scotia to propose ..."

Rachel was starting to grasp the level of manipulation going on here. Mother and son had planned all this in minute detail. "Yes, Vanessa, I—"

"And you turned him down?"

"Well, not lightly, I—"

"You have made a huge mistake, girl."

Vanessa had hired Rachel as a junior editor while she was still in university. That was twenty years ago. The owner had always treated her well, until now. But Rachel was not going to take this. She was forty. Rachel flushed. "Hold it now."

"No, you hold it. Are you still pursuing that author, that Logan Stewart?" Vanessa raised her voice, looking like a volcano about to blow.

Rachel assumed that she meant for the book. "Yes."

"Once you presented that book in the board room, it became *our* project, *our* property. Have Nicholas or I approved your trip to Nova Scotia to offer Stewart a contract?"

"No, I—"

"Then stop. Full stop. *We* will handle all negotiations from now on. If you continue to pursue this, there will be legal consequences."

"What are you talking about?"

"You heard me. Be careful, or it could lead to your dismissal. And it could affect your pension plan with the firm."

Rachel was shocked. She hadn't planned on losing her job, and she didn't know if Vanessa's words were just idle threats. She needed to speak with Lena. Lena's brother was an attorney and sometimes gave

Rachel advice.

Vanessa continued: "And there are other changes coming to Big Apple, and soon. Big changes. I want you in my office tomorrow morning. Do I make myself clear?"

Rachel felt trapped. "Yes, ma'am ... but how ..?"

"You will fly back immediately with Nicholas. I have called all department heads to a big meeting tomorrow."

Rachel glanced at Nick, who turned away. *Coward.* She could kick herself, *and* Nick *and* Vanessa. How had she gotten herself into this position? How had she not seen this coming? The obvious thing to do was quit, but she was not fully prepared for that. She would need access to all her funds if she was to pursue her dream, and that included her company pension. Would they play hard ball with her? It sure looked like it at the moment. She'd have to sell the condo. She had to get back to New York and get things settled asap. She thought of Logan and what she'd promised him just a short time ago. She felt like a traitor, but she had no choice. "Okay." The call ended.

A half hour later, she sat in the lobby. She checked her passport, although she probably wouldn't need it. She looked for her phone to call Bree, but couldn't find it. She panicked a bit, searching every pocket and her purse, but still couldn't locate it. Sitting in her chair and feeling defeated, her eyes welled up.

A few minutes later, she heard Nick walking towards

her. She quickly wiped her tears and stood up. Two male pilots and a stewardess joined them.

"Are we ready?" Nick asked.

"Yes, sir," answered the captain. "We need to leave immediately, as a snowstorm is going to hit the northeast soon."

They walked out to the waiting taxis. The pilots took the first one, and she and Nick the second. She sat in the front.

Logan was beyond frustrated, sitting on the couch sipping a coffee. An hour had passed and still no word from Rachel.

Bree poked her head in from the kitchen. "Should I make supper?"

"May as well," replied Mark. "Are you staying, Da?"

"I guess so. Do you want to try her number again?" Logan asked Bree. She'd already tried a few times, but couldn't reach her.

Bree stood in the opening to the living room and called Rachel again. She frowned and left another message. "I'm sure she wouldn't go back to New York without telling us."

"This is so strange," commented Mark, sitting in his chair.

Logan frowned. He was trying to keep his head this time, and believe in Rachel. There's no way she would make him that promise and then break it. He needed to have patience and wisdom.

Bree addressed them: "I think I'll make some burgers and fries. How does that sound?"

"Sounds good to me," answered Mark. "I'll set the table."

"Sound good," said Logan.

During a very quiet supper, Bree tried to phone twice again, with no success. "I'm getting worried about her," she said.

"Yeah, me too," replied Logan.

"I think we need to relax," said Mark. "We have no real indication that anything bad has happened. Maybe she's having an intense meeting with Nick. She's a top editor at a major firm. I think she can handle herself."

Bree reached for his hand. "You're probably right, Honey."

After supper, they returned to the living room. Bree served banana bread and settled down on the love seat between Logan and Mark.

The dessert didn't make Logan feel any better, though, as each half hour without hearing from Rachel just added to his growing anxiety.

Bree cleared her throat. "Da, there's something I need to tell you."

Uh-oh, thought Logan. "What?"

"Rachel told me a bit more about Nick, when she first arrived yesterday. She told me not to say anything for now, but because of what's transpiring, I think I should tell you."

Logan leaned forward on the couch. "Go ahead."

"Well, when Rachel returned to New York last time, he bought her flowers and then invited her out to dinner."

"They had a date?"

"Yes — well, it wasn't a date per se. It was a business meal. Anyway, Nick expressed interest in her and made some big offer. But she turned him down."

Logan, rubbed his jaw. "So, what are we to think — he's trying again?"

Bree's eyebrows raised. "I don't know. Maybe."

"Hmm. She didn't tell me any of that on the way in. In fact, we expressed feelings for each other."

"Really?" asked Mark. "That's great."

"Is it though?" answered Logan. "Women."

"Hey!" said Bree.

"Sorry, Bree. Just kidding."

Logan felt tired and exasperated. It had been a long day. Actually, it had been a great day before Nick showed up. He stood up and stretched his arms. "Well, I'm heading home. Thanks for everything, Bree. Let me know if and when she makes contact."

"I will, Da."

Logan drove home, shaking his head most of the way. "I'll never understand women," he muttered to himself. Why would Rachel leave with Nick, if she did? Maybe he still had some kind of hold over her. Maybe she secretly loved him. Logan tried to fight against these negative thoughts, but it was hard. All she had to do was tell Nick off and get a taxi back, or call Bree or himself. They would've come and gotten her. No, as far as he was concerned there was no good reason that she hadn't phoned. It smacked of weak character. It smacked of Carly.

Logan had called Carly after he'd found the note. She finally answered his call after a couple of days of trying. She told him she loved him, but couldn't live in Cape Breton. She was an Alberta girl. A Calgary girl, to be specific. And all her friends and family lived there. She invited him to come visit her, but in the end he had decided not to.

He turned up White's Lane.

In his mind, Carly's reluctance to live with him in Cape Breton meant that she didn't love him enough. How could she choose a place over a person? If *he* truly loved someone, he could live with them anywhere. But he wasn't going back to Calgary. Heck, it wasn't just him. He'd convinced Mark and Bree to move down also. Nope, he was going to stay in the Cape, even if he had to live forever by himself in Low Point. He had everything he needed up there.

Well, he *thought* he had everything he needed, until Rachel showed up. She had rocked his world. And now, here he was again, with woman trouble. How did he get himself into these messes? He pulled up to the house and turned the truck to face the ocean. He shut off the engine and gazed out the window, placing his keys and phone on the seat beside him.

His thoughts turned to Mark's mom, Taylor, his

first real love. He had met her at a club. He smiled. They used to dance up a storm. She'd been quite a free spirit. Too free. But she'd given him a great gift. Mark. They both loved Mark to pieces. Mark was still in some sort of contact with her, whenever she popped up — almost always in a new city. Still partying.

In hindsight, Carly was the rebound relationship. He'd heard enough chatter on those radio talk shows to know that basic psychology. Other podcasts and internet shows had also given him an education on the fairer sex. So, he'd tried to honestly look at himself. Maybe *he* was the problem. Or at least half of it. He agreed with that. His parents had abandoned him with his grandmother at two years of age. She'd raised him by herself in Low Point, New Waterford and Scotchtown. She had been a good Christian woman, although a bit strict. They attended the United Church every Sunday.

However, he knew that his wild side had something to do with his parents neglect of him. He started drinking and smoking around sixteen, and graduated to pot by the time he left town and joined the Air Force. Thankfully, he'd settled down, years later, working with the oil companies. They had a strict *no drugs* policy, which he was now thankful for. He still had a couple of beers now and then, but the crazy nights were far behind him.

After Carly was gone for good, he tried to enjoy life again, although it was a bit lonely on the hill. Whenever he felt depressed, he popped in to Mark and Bree's, or dropped by the shop. They were always there for him. They knew he was struggling after Carly.

So, everything was perfectly fine until Rachel showed up. And, although, he'd sworn off women, at least for a while — she'd changed all that. She was incredibly beautiful. It was hard to believe she would be interested in someone like him. Not only stunning, she was smart and caring — everything a man could possibly want. He was falling for her big time. She even forgave his big stumble at Daniel's Alehouse. She was wonderful. He'd thought about shopping for a ring, but then remembered that she wanted to take it slow. Now this. How was he supposed to process this Nick thing?

He was confused.

Was she weak? Was she weak? He couldn't help but think so. Carly had been weak. He had thought Rachel was strong, but maybe he was wrong. He shook his head for the millionth time, grabbed his keys and left the vehicle. He unlocked the door, threw his keys on the table and sat in his chair in the living room. It was freezing. He started a fire and looked out the window. He recalled Rachel's first visit. She had sat right there and looked out this window. He had gazed at her intelligent blue eyes as she'd studied the ocean. It's possible that he'd started to fall in love with her at that very moment.

He walked into the kitchen and got the stove going.

He would have a nice hot cup of tea and think things through. He'd also say a prayer for Rachel. Who knew what was really happening with her and Nick. Only God knew. A part of him said to trust her. She had promised to return after all.

Mark asked Bree to try again. Still nothing.

Suddenly, Mark snapped his fingers and stood up. "Phone again," he said, as he bolted out of the room.

Bree raised her eyebrows and called again. A minute later, Mark walked into the living room holding up a phone that was lit up.

"Oh my God," said Bree.

"Yup. She muted it when we played cards. Remember? It was on the floor on the far side of the bed."

Bree phoned Logan right away, but there was no answer. She left a message.

Early the next morning, Bree turned on her laptop and discovered eight short Facebook messages from Rachel:

Lost my phone! :(
Had to fly back to NY. Sorry! <3
Big changes at work.
Job on the line.
Nick proposed. Said NO!
Did I forget my phone at your place?
Will call soon with new number. <3

What is your phone number again? <3

"Yay! Rachel's in contact!"

"Really?"

"Yes, she sent me some messages. She's in New York, or home in Connecticut. She's going to call soon."

"Wow. They must have threatened her, eh?"

"Nick proposed, but she shot him down."

"Oh, wow. Call Da and let him know."

She called him again, but there was still no answer.

Mark looked out the living room window. The storm had started.

9

Big Apple Bites

Rachel was exhausted, having barely slept. She'd finally gotten home to Stamford around eight at night and fell asleep on the couch. Before that, she'd fired off a few messages to Bree.

Early the next morning, Rachel walked into her office with two small boxes and secretly started to pack personal belongings, just in case. She was going to be ready for *anything*, including being terminated. She knew she had to move, and fast.

A half hour later, Mel entered the outer office and turned the lights on. As Rachel slid her boxes behind a cabinet, Mel stepped into her office wearing a pink pantsuit with a white top and heels.

"You're back!" exclaimed Mel.

Rachel sat down. "Yeah, not by my choice."

"Why? What happened?"

Rachel spoke in hushed tones. "Nick flew into Cape Breton and proposed, for one thing."

"*Really*?"

Rachel nodded. "Yes. I turned him down, of course, but then Vanessa got on the phone and demanded that I return, immediately. Big meeting this morning."

"Yeah, I know."

Rachel gazed at Mel from head to toe. "Hey, what happened to your glasses? And did you get a new do?"

"Yeah, just wearing my contacts. I got them a while ago, but ..."

"Either way, you look stunning."

She smiled. "Thanks."

"And your hair looks lovely. Did you put some streaks in?"

Mel twirled, playing with her hair. "Yeah. Like it?"

"*Love it*! Want to get together tonight?"

"Um, actually, I'm not feeling that well. Been a bit under the weather the past few days."

"Oh, sorry. Well, maybe in a few days."

"Sure."

Rachel lowered her voice. "By the way, the Dragon Lady said big changes are coming. Be prepared."

Mel frowned. "Yeah, you can feel it. I should get to work. Got lots of typing to get done."

"Okay. Also, I might be selling my condo. Let me know if you hear of anyone looking."

Mel's eyes popped. "You're moving?"

"Don't know yet. Just keeping all my options open. Keep it under your hat."

Mel turned to leave. "Of course."

A few minutes later, Rachel's desk phone rang. "Hi, Lena."

"Hey. How was Cape Breton?"

"The Dragon Lady summoned me back," she whispered.

"I heard. Can you pop over to my office?"

"Sure. Be right there."

"Got a coffee?"

"Yep."

Rachel strolled into her office, and sat down in one of the big chairs in front of Lena's desk. "What, what?"

"Close the door."

She did and sat back down.

Lena finished typing something on her keyboard, removed her glasses, and sat back. "Well, maybe it's nothing, but I saw Mel coming out of Nick's office the other day. Her clothes were ruffled and she was adjusting her skirt. She didn't notice me and took the elevator back down."

Rachel was stunned. "Are you kidding me?"

"Nope. Wanted you to know. And, of course, you've seen her makeover?"

Rachel took a sip of coffee as she stared at Lena and started to connect the dots. "Oh my goodness. You know, now that I think about it, there have been some things. Like things I told her that Nick somehow knew."

Lena nodded her head. "Vanessa has called everyone

in today. Zach was already on vacation, like you. He's not impressed."

"Wow. I have to see her at nine. I'm secretly packing my personal belongings. I brought in two boxes."

Lena shook her head. "Rumours are swirling."

"Yes. By the way, can Big Apple keep my pension if I quit or for any other reason?"

"Nope. They can't touch it. Our pension sits with a third party overseeing it. Why, has she been threatening you?"

"Yes, sort of. She also said I can't pursue the Logan Stewart books. I think she's going to fire me."

"Her loss. Any firm in the city would hire you immediately."

Rachel reached across the desk and held her hand. "Thanks, friend."

"Anytime. That's what friends are for."

"Yeah, *real* friends. Gotta go."

"Keep me posted. If you need anything, call. Otherwise, see you at ten."

"Actually, can I use your cell for a minute. I left mine somewhere. I need to call someone in Cape Breton and let them know I'm okay."

"Of course." Lena grabbed her phone and handed it to Rachel, who called Bree.

At nine o'clock, Rachel sat outside Vanessa Hoffman's office on the top floor. She could hear the owner's raised voice behind the closed door. Rachel imagined her with fire coming out of her mouth and smoke rising out of her nostrils. A few minutes later, a red and flustered Aiden exited and blew past her on the way to the elevator. He might have been in tears. Well, this should be fun.

The receptionist ushered her in.

The Dragon Lady sat behind an oversized wooden desk, caked in make-up, and decked out in a bright red blazer over a white shirt. A gaudy pearl necklace and long sparkly earrings finished off her look.

Rachel sat down.

Vanessa eye's narrowed as she stared at her. "I won't rehash things from yesterday, but suffice it to say that I consider your recent actions to be reprehensible. You can no longer keep your position as the acquisitions editor. Let me know if you are interested in staying at the firm, by working in another department, for lesser pay, or if you wish to resign." Quite satisfied with herself, she grinned and leaned back in her chair, looking like the cat who swallowed the canary. "Is it your intention to resign? I heard that you're selling your condo."

How could she possibly know that already? Rachel had only told Mel. *So that confirms it. Mel is indeed a traitor. How long has she been seeing Nick behind my back? I would have wished her well. But giving my secret plans to Nick ... to Vanessa?*

"I don't know yet," answered Rachel. She felt her face getting red and stood. "Is that all?" She needed time to bounce everything off Lena, so didn't want to tip her hand, just yet.

"Yes. And I want everyone at the ten a.m. meeting."

Rachel nodded and left. She made a point to stop by Lena's office and update her.

At ten o'clock, Rachel walked into the meeting room. The room was filled with department heads and their assistants. Mel and Nick were conspicuous by their absence. The tension was palpable; fear on many faces. No one's job was safe. She sat in the same chair she'd sat on a million times. Would this be the last time? Vanessa sat at the head of the table, scowling.

After everyone had taken their seats, Vanessa cleared her throat. "Thank you all for attending and a special thanks to those who returned from an early Christmas break. I have some important announcements. First, my son, Nicholas, will be taking my place as owner and CEO, effective immediately, and will be running the day to day operations, such as he has done the past few months. I expect you to give him your full support and cooperation." Most heads nodded in agreement.

Rachel glanced at Lena, who looked back at her with raised eyebrows.

Vanessa picked up a piece of paper, read it and then put it back down. "Rachel Abrams and Aiden Gooden will be stepping down from their positions. We thank them for their years of service. The new department heads will be in place when we return in January." Gasps filled the room, but no one who still wanted a job said anything.

Eyes stared at the two who had been unceremoniously dumped. Rachel sat stoically with a thin smile etched on her face. Lena smiled at her. Her support was everything.

Vanessa shuffled in her seat. "I have one more announcement. But before I do, does anyone have anything to add?"

No one did.

Vanessa intertwined her fingers and grinned from ear to ear. "I would like to announce the engagement of my son, Nicholas Hoffman, to Melanie Young. At that moment, the couple walked into the room, Nick beaming and Mel forcing a half-smile and avoiding eye contact with Rachel.

Even though she suspected something like this, Rachel was still astonished. The couple actually looked great together. She was the perfect girl for Nick. With her good looks, curves, and big hair, she'd look great in a mini skirt, sitting in his bright-red Corvette. *Enjoy your mansion and big cars. And try not to think about what he's doing when out of town on business trips.* Rachel would have felt sorry for her, if she hadn't turned into such a Judas.

A couple of people started to clap, and then most joined Vanessa in growing applause and cheers. Everyone, except Rachel, Lena and Zach. The newly engaged couple joined Vanessa at the head of the table, still standing and smiling.

Vanessa's plan was obviously to humiliate Rachel.

She took this as her cue, and rose to leave.

"Where are you going?" barked Vanessa. "This meeting is not over."

"It is for me. I quit."

Gasps filled the room again.

"And so do I!" yelled Lena, erupting from her chair and joining Rachel at the doorway.

"This is outrageous!" hollered Vanessa, grabbing her phone. "Send security to the third floor," she bellowed into it. "We have a couple of ex-employees who need an immediate escort out."

Lena's face turned red. "You are *disgusting*, you old hag! They lay one hand on either of us and I'll sue you into oblivion."

All eyes turned to Vanessa, who looked like she'd been shot by a canon, falling back in her seat and holding her chest as if she was having a heart attack.

She looked up at her son. "Nicholas, are you going to just stand there? *Do something*!"

Lena grinned. "Yeah, do something Nick. My brother, *the attorney*, would just *love* to take you on."

Nick didn't move.

Mel started to cry.

Lena put her arm around Rachel as they marched out the door and down the hallway. "Got an extra box? I've got to grab a few possessions."

Rachel laughed. "Yeah. Are you coming over tonight for a glass of bubbly?"

"Oh, yeah!" They fist-bumped and walked to their

respective offices.

10

The Blizzard

On the afternoon of December twentieth, Mark was checking a string of Christmas lights, when his phone rang. It was a New York area code.

"Hi Mark. It's Rachel. I'm truly sorry for how things turned out, for the way I left."

"It's okay, Rachel. Bree told me you messaged and called her."

"Good. I will explain everything that happened soon, but the main reason I called is that I'm worried about Logan."

"Da? Why?"

"Well, I know the big storm has started. I've been watching it on the news. I tried to call Logan a couple of times to explain why I left, but I can't get a hold of him. I then called Bree, but couldn't get a hold of her, either."

"I think she's doing laundry and charging her phone. She's in the basement."

"Oh, okay."

"Maybe Da doesn't want to talk to you right now."

"I wouldn't blame him. Have you spoken to him recently?"

"No, but he's not always tied to his phone, either." Mark walked into the living room and looked out the window. "It's been snowing most of the day. There's at least two feet out there."

"What time is it there?"

"Just about 4:30. Pretty dark."

"Hmm."

"I'll try to reach him and call you back. Is this your new number?"

"Yes, thanks, Mark, and I apologize again for the way I left. I probably should have stayed and handled things better ... I got fired today. Everything is up in the air right now, but I'm planning to get back to Cape Breton as soon as I can."

"You lost your job?"

"Yes. I stood up to Nick and his mother. And that's the price I paid."

"Sorry to hear that. I'll get back to you soon."

"Okay."

He called his dad, but it tried to go to the answering service. However, the robotic female voice told him it was full. Mark got a bad feeling. He called again. Same thing.

Just then, Bree came up from the basement and walked through the kitchen. He turned and gazed at her.

"What's wrong?" she asked.

He explained everything. "I think I'm going to take a shot out to Da's, just to make sure he's okay."

She walked over to him and stared out the window. "Are you sure? It's getting worse. There's two feet of snow already on the ground, and higher drifts."

"I'll take the ski-doo."

"The *ski-doo?* Are you crazy? Da's probably fine. Now, I'll have to worry about the both of you."

He hugged her. "Don't worry, Honey, I'll be okay. I have a bad feeling about this. Something's wrong. I have to go."

She frowned. "Okay, well go then. I'd never forgive myself if something happened to Da."

"Good. I'll get ready then. Mark took his boots, went to the basement and got dressed quickly in his snowsuit, ski mask and big mitts. He then grabbed his helmet and went back upstairs. Sneaking into the bedroom, he took his switchblade out of the night stand and put it in a zipped up pocket — just in case.

He went out the back to the shed and uncovered the yellow-and-black ski-doo, driving it into the front yard. He checked the gas level. Everything was good. When he was ready, he banged on the front door.

Bree opened it and they embraced. She shivered. "Wow, it's so cold with that wind." She looked him in the eyes. "Be safe, Mark. I'll be praying the whole time."

"Thanks, Babe. Keep your phone charged. I'll call you as soon as I'm there. And if you hear anything, call me right away."

"I will. Love you."

"Love you, too." The wind was swirling as Mark started up the ski-doo and pulled down his visor. He waved to Bree who waved out the window. He was soon on the highway, and thankfully, it was empty. The snow flurries played havoc with his sight as he picked up speed, but he made good time. Soon, he was turning right on White's Lane and heading up the hill. The snow was pristine, but he made out a couple of tire tracks.

The snowfall became a full blizzard as he drove up the twisty-turny road. Just before the last long curve he saw Da's truck to the side of the road. *What the—* It was blanketed with two inches of snow, the doors closed. The Chevy looked like it had hit a small tree just off the road and was stuck. "*Oh, God.*"

Mark shut off the ski-doo and hopped off, trudging through knee-high snow to the truck. He threw open the passenger door. No Da, but blood spots on the steering wheel. "Damn." Da's phone was lying on the floor. He grabbed it. Closing the door, he walked to the front of the truck and surveyed the damage. The grill and hood were dented — the tree embedded a little. The left front tire was buried. He guessed the rear one was also.

Taking a mini-flashlight out of his arm pocket, he

turned it on. He pointed it down and saw his father's footprints in the snow, heading up the road. He jumped on the snowmobile, started it up and drove around the last curve. As he slowed down, he noticed a few animal tracks beside his father's footprints and a few blood spots. *"What the hell?"*

As he approached the house, the security lights came on. He shut off the ski-doo and looked towards the small barn. Staring at him were two large dogs. No — *coyotes* — snarling and barking. Mark reached for his knife as they bolted for him. The first one knocked him backwards and tried to bite his face — crashing his teeth against the visor. Mark reached for the knife which had fallen onto the footrest. He clutched it and pressed the button, opening the blade, as the second coyote bit into his leg. He screamed, grabbed the beast and stabbed it repeatedly. The other coyote took off into the woods.

Mark rose to his feet and kicked the coyote lying in the snow, making sure it was dead. He looked down at his snowsuit, which was ripped — his thigh throbbing in pain. He trudged up to the door and walked inside, closing the door behind him. "Da! Da!" He shouted.

"In here."

A trail of blood spots went from the pantry to the coal stove. He rushed into the living room, where Da sat in his chair, holding a cloth to his nose.

Mark leaned down and put a hand on his shoulder. "Are you okay? What happened?"

"I was attempting to drive to your place, but the roads were in bad shape, so turned back. I was just stupid, trying to find the darn phone that was ringing. When I looked back up, I smashed into a tree. I banged my nose off the steering wheel. The truck was stuck, so I walked up the road. I noticed two coyotes stalking me. One attacked and bit my hand. He held it up. I just made it inside."

Mark grabbed another cloth from the kitchen and wrapped his dad's hand. "I just ran into those damn coyotes outside. One attacked me."

"Oh, God, are you okay?"

"Yeah, I killed one and the other one ran into the woods."

"Good man!"

Mark bent down. "Any other injuries?"

"Well, I've got a killer headache. Why don't you put a fire on."

"A *fire*? Da, you're going to the hospital." He looked into his eyes. "You might have a concussion. I just have to call Bree. Everyone is worried about you."

"Who's everyone?"

"Well, Rachel is the one who alerted us to the fact you were missing."

"Rachel?"

"Yeah, she's been trying to reach you for some time."

"Hmm."

Mark smiled. "Yeah — I think she likes you. I need

some rope."

"In the pantry."

"By the way, where was your phone all this time?"

"I forgot it in the truck last night. It was dead today when I found it. Tried to charge it a little ..."

"Da, you need to keep your phone on you and charged, especially living up here."

"Yeah, I guess so."

While looking around the pantry, Mark called 911 and told them to expect them at the Sydney hospital. Within a few minutes, he found the rope. He then called his wife. "Hi, Bree. I'm at Da's. He's alive, but had an accident on White's Lane. I think he has a broken nose and maybe a concussion. I'm going to bring him to the hospital. We also got attacked by coyotes. One bit Da on the hand. One attacked me and bit my leg, but it's dead."

"Oh my God, Mark! *Coyotes*? Are you okay?"

"Yeah, in a bit of pain, but I'm going to drive us to Sydney hospital. Already called 911 and let them know. Call Rachel and fill her in. Love you."

"Okay, love you, too. Praying for you and Da. Please be careful."

Mark walked back to the living room. "Alright, Da, let's get you on the ski-doo."

"The *ski-doo*?"

Mark laughed. "Yup."

Wearing Logan's jacket, Rachel was lying on

the couch when the phone rang. "Thank God." She grabbed it off the coffee table and sat up. "Hi, Bree."

"Are you sitting down?"

"Yes, on the couch. Why?"

"Da was in an accident."

"What? An accident?"

"Yes, he's okay, he's alive. But Mark thinks he might have a broken nose and a concussion."

"*Oh my God.*"

"There's more. They were attacked by coyotes."

"*Coyotes*? What the hell are they? Like wolves?"

"Yeah, like wolves. The ones here are big. Anyway. Da was bitten on the hand and Mark on the leg. I think Mark killed one of them."

"Oh my God! This can't be real."

"Yeah, I know. Mark went out on the ski-doo. He's now driving both of them to the hospital."

Rachel started to cry. "This is all my fault. If I hadn't left, none of this would've happened."

"It's not your fault, Rachel. It's not. Come on now. I need you."

"And I need you." Tears rolled down Rachel's cheeks. "What am I going to do?"

"We're going to pray. That's what I'm doing."

"You're right. That's what Mom would do."

"When can you return?"

"Let me check online and get right back to you."

"Okay. We love you, Rachel."

"Love you, too, Bree. What would I do without you?

Keep your phone close."

"I will."

Rachel put her phone on the coffee table and paced around the condo. *I need something. Wine or coffee?* She decided on tea and put the kettle on. She took a minute in the kitchen and said a quick prayer for Logan and Mark. When was the last time she'd prayed for anyone, for anything? She pictured her mom in her mind. Her strong, compassionate hazel eyes. Rachel smiled. Mom was a prayer warrior. She was always praying. Rachel hadn't kept that legacy, that's for sure. She hadn't kept much from her small-town life at all. No, she'd become a big city girl.

She walked back into the living room. She couldn't sit. She wished the water would hurry up. Why, oh why, did this have to happen? Was not life crazy enough for her lately? She looked up. *What are you doing, God?* At least she could blame *Him*. She paced. She paced. She had just found the man she wanted to spend the rest of her life with. Her kindred spirit. And now he's on his way to the hospital. Attacked by coyotes. *Oh my God. Coyotes.* Was it not enough that he'd been in an accident?

Realizing it could have been a lot worse, she looked up again. "Thank you, Lord," she whispered. She tapped her chin with a finger. *What to do? What to do?* She turned on her laptop at the kitchen table and made her tea. *I need to get a flight.*

"*Ugh!*" The first thing she noticed was news about the

snowstorm and cancelled flights in the northeast. She went to the Weather Network and looked up Sydney, Nova Scotia. *Great.* Tons of snow falling tonight and tomorrow. It was going to take a couple of days to get there. *Fantastic.* The one thing she didn't have in this situation was patience. She realized the persona she'd built up in New York was useless. Rachel, the independent woman. The big acquisitions editor. The fashionista. All utterly useless right now. She wished her mother was still alive. How she missed her and Dad. They were all about character. She'd become all about appearances.

She sipped her tea. At least she had Bree and Lena. True friends. She'd call them both again shortly. She was going to do everything in her power to get back to the man she loved asap. She was going to make everything right. She was going to solve her life here and there. She returned to the couch and hugged a pillow. *God help me.*

Bree was watching out the window, when the snowmobile sped up the driveway. Opening the door, she hugged Mark tight at the entrance. "*My hero.*" They kissed and she helped him out of his snowsuit. It was torn and had blood stains on it, so she threw it outside, to the side of the steps. Back inside, she looked down at his ripped jeans and saw a white bandage underneath. "How's your leg, Honey?"

"It's okay. They cleaned it and put in three stitches.

But it's sore."

"How's Da?"

"Good. Slight concussion. Nose is *not* broken, thank God. Two stitches in his hand. We both had to get tetanus shots for the damn coyotes."

"Oh my God. This is so crazy."

"Yup." With Bree helping, he limped to his chair and sat down.

"Can I get you a beer or coffee?"

"Coffee, please."

Bree went to the kitchen and returned, handing him a warm cup. "I still can't believe it, Mark. *Coyotes*?"

"I know, but we've been warning about them for years now."

"So, they're keeping Da overnight?"

"Yeah. And hopefully the snow will stop soon, so I can get him. The roads will have to be plowed."

"Well, the news is better than I expected. His nose isn't broken and only a couple stitches."

"Yeah, not so bad."

She shook her head. "Rachel freaked out when I told her about the accident and the coyotes."

"I bet. You should update her."

At seven o'clock the following evening, Lena popped over for a visit.

"Sorry for cancelling yesterday," Rachel said, as they sat on the sectional.

"I totally understand. What happened?"

"Logan got in a small accident in the snowstorm and then when he had to walk up the hill to his house, he got attacked by coyotes. I still can't believe it."

Lena hugged her.

"But there is a silver lining. Bree, his daughter-in-law phoned me back and told me his injuries are not as bad as feared. Thank God! He only has a slight concussion and two stitches in his hand."

Lena smiled. "Well, that's good news. If you think about it, guys get hurt in sports all the time. You should see some of the injuries at the Rangers games."

Rachel chuckled. "Are you still going to those hockey games?"

"Oh, yeah. I love it. Nothing like a good fight after a hard day's work."

Rachel laughed. "Oh, Lena, you're totally crazy! But you make me feel a lot better about this." She jumped up. "Coffee or champagne?"

"Well, if you're sad, coffee. But if you're happy that Logan's injuries aren't so bad, then champagne."

Rachel returned with two glasses and the bottle she had on ice.

"Yay!" shouted Lena.

Rachel popped it and poured them each a glass.

Lena raised her glass. "To Logan."

"And to Mark, his son — who went out on his snowmobile and got him and who was also bitten by a coyote."

"Are you kidding me?"

Rachel frowned. "Nope. He was bit in the leg and got stitches too."

"Oh my goodness. Is Cape Breton filled with wild beasts?"

Rachel laughed. "No, not really."

"Good. Anyway, you better not move there. You better stay here, close to me."

"Ha, ha. We'll see."

Lena raised her eyebrows. "So, tell me all about Logan the Canadian."

"Well, he's handsome, quiet, strong, *and* ... a writer."

"Yeah, *and*?"

"The time apart did us good. When I returned for Christmas, I realized how bad I was falling for him. When he gazes at me with his piercing green eyes from underneath those long brown bangs, my knees get weak. He's so good looking." She fanned her face with her hand.

"Ooh. You're heading into steamy romance territory."

They chuckled.

Rachel gazed at her. "I wish."

"Oh, there hasn't been any ..."

"No, not yet. I actually *dissuaded* him from moving too fast. Now I regret it."

Lena lifted her glass. They clinked and both took another big gulp.

Lena grinned. "Well, you're going to have to *persuade* him to get going. Is he your *Mr. Darcy*?"

"No, but he might be my *Captain Wentworth*."

"Ah. Nice."

"Yeah, and now, after this latest crisis, all I want to do is get back there asap. I'm trying for the twenty-third." Rachel topped up their drinks. "I love him, Lena."

"I can see that."

Rachel sighed. "When we talk about writing and books, I feel like he's an old friend. My kindred spirit. I could talk with him for hours on end."

"Okay, well we have to get you back there."

"Thanks, friend."

They both leaned forward and hugged again.

"You're welcome. Now let's talk about business before you go."

Rachel frowned. "Yes, the other crisis in my life."

Lena grinned. "But wasn't today liberating? Wasn't it nice to tell off the Dragon Lady and storm out? It was one of the most exhilarating experiences of my life."

Rachel laughed. "Lena you're a riot."

"Wasn't it, fun, though?"

"Yes, it was. It was so nice to quit and walk out. It was liberating indeed."

Lena grinned. "Did you see Aiden's face when the old hag demoted him?"

"Oh my goodness!" said Rachel, laughing. "He finally got his."

"Yep. So, what are we going to do?"

"I've always wanted to have my own firm."

Lena smiled. "*So* interesting. Are you looking for a partner?"

"Are you kidding me?"

Lena arched her eyebrows and stared at her.

Rachel took a swig of her drink. "Okay. Where would our office be?"

"How about right here in Stamford? Wouldn't have to do the ugly commute into the City anymore. At least, not every day. I'm sure we'd have some meetings there."

"That would be Heaven."

"Yeah. You could do Acquisitions and I could do Publicity."

Rachel tapped a finger on her chin. "We could hire someone for Sales and Marketing."

Lena took a sip of her drink. "I could talk to Zach. He was steaming today."

Rachel grinned. "You think he'd join us? That would be marvellous."

"Yeah, *marvellous*."

Rachel raised her eyebrows. "Um, weren't you crushing on him, at one time."

"Yeah, and I still do. I think he's my only chance to prevent me from becoming an old maid."

Rachel chuckled. "C'mon, Lena, you're smart and pretty. Lots of guys would love to have a girl like you."

"Where are they? Actually, I'm getting old*er*, am tall and skinny and haven't had a date in forever."

"Aw." Rachel leaned over and they hugged.

Lena gazed at her. "Zach is shy and kind of goofy, but he's also handsome and brilliant."

"Well, as co-owner, I order you to call him and invite him to a meeting."

Lena grinned. "Good idea."

11

Let's Try Again

On December twenty-third, Logan, Mark and Bree sat in the living room, enjoying tea, coffee, blueberry scones and the warmth of the fire. Christmas music played and Christmas lights twinkled.

Logan, with a bandaged hand, and Mark, sat on the couch facing Bree, who knelt on the floor, surrounded by old Christmas cards from years gone by. She'd been reading them, but stopped and looked at the men. "I still can't believe you two were attacked by coyotes. We need to be very thankful your injuries weren't far worse."

Mark softly rubbed his leg. "Yup, from now on, the only good coyote is a dead coyote."

"I agree," said Logan. "I used to defend them all the time, but now they're just a dangerous nuisance."

"Anyone want another beer?" asked Bree, rising to her feet.

"Yes, please," the men answered in unison.

Car lights in the driveway, caught Bree's attention. Ignoring them, she smiled and grabbed the drinks. She returned and handed them out, as the doorbell rang.

"Who can that be?" asked Mark, craning his head to see out the window. All he saw was a taxi turning back onto the highway.

At that moment, Bree was already opening the door. The women embraced.

"*Oh my God*!" exclaimed Logan. "What are you doing here?"

Mark just sat in stunned silence and gazed at Bree — who grinned at him. Bree hung up Rachel's coat and strolled into the living room, waving for Rachel to come in. Rachel removed her boots and walked into the middle of the room.

"Mark, can you help me in the kitchen, please?" Bree asked.

"Sure." He rose, and quickly hugged Rachel as he passed by.

Rachel, wearing a dark-blue pantsuit with a white blouse, gazed at Logan. "I know I hurt you by leaving the way I did, but I felt I had no choice at the time. I want to tell you everything that transpired since then, and I want you to wait until the very end before saying anything."

"Okay."

"Nick proposed to me at the hotel with a giant diamond. With the offer came a life of luxury and becoming co-owner of Big Apple. I turned him down."

A smile crept onto Logan's face.

"His mother, Vanessa, then threatened my job and pension on a phone call, right after that. So, it seemed coordinated. She demanded that I return to New York immediately. She also threatened to harm your books. So, I knew I had to return and settle things once and for all. I lost my phone in the chaos of that day, so couldn't phone you or Bree.

"Once I was back, Vanessa called me into her office, where she demoted me. I then found out that my best friend and assistant, Melanie, was the new acquisitions editor. In a subsequent meeting, with all department heads present, I was humiliated further, when Vanessa announced that Nick and Mel were engaged to be married. I quit on the spot.

"I rushed home and put my condo on the market and tried to think of everything that was in front of me. I ... I ... Rachel's eyes welled up.

Logan stood. "*Rachel.*"

"And then the horrible call from Bree. You were in an accident and attacked by coyotes." She gazed at his bandaged hand and black eyes. "Are you okay? How is your hand? Is your nose sore?" She started to cry.

Logan rushed to her. "My nose is tender and my hand is sore. But, other than that, I'm fine."

She gazed up at him through moist eyes, as he wrapped his arms around her. She buried her head into his chest, pulling him even closer. "Can you forgive me for leaving that day?"

"Of course. Bree told me everything. You've done nothing wrong. That owner sounds like a witch."

Rachel chuckled. "Oh, she is. We call her the *Dragon Lady.*"

"I will admit I was upset and confused that day. I knew Nick was going to try something like that. I could feel it. I was angry when hours passed without hearing from you ..."

She looked up. "I should have listened to you and Bree. It was one of the biggest mistakes of my life. You must have been so hurt."

"She really threatened to harm my books?"

Rachel sniffled. "Yes."

He gazed deep into her eyes. "Is there anything you need from me right now? Money? Anything?"

She smiled. "I need a tissue."

Bree jumped into the living room and handed Rachel a box of tissues.

"Thanks, Bree. That girl is wonderful."

Logan smiled. "Yes, she is."

"I just need your understanding and support. The last thing I wanted, especially on that day, was to hurt you."

"I'm okay, especially now. There's nothing I want more on this Earth than to be with you. How did you get here? There are no flights from Halifax to Sydney in December."

"I met an older Cape Breton lady at the car rental counter in Halifax. She was renting, but was concerned with prices. We started talking and decided to rent a car together. It was incredible. Another miracle."

Logan shook his head. "*You are amazing.* You said no to Nick, quit your job, saved my books and somehow made it back in time for Christmas."

She raised a hand and softly brushed his stubbly cheek. "Does this hurt?"

"No, it feels good." He glanced at her lips and lowered his head. She stood on her tip-toes, her hands running through his hair. Her lips parted. He leaned into her as she pulled his head down, her heart racing. Their lips met. She couldn't remember what they'd been talking about. She only knew that she was in love. That he was the one. The one she wanted to be with forever. The sweet kiss lasted a long time. As her mind settled down, she realized that Logan's lips tasted extra sweet.

"Um. You taste like blueberries."

He laughed. "Bree served us scones ten minutes ago."

"Hmm." She gazed into his eyes and licked her lips. "I love blueberries."

"And I love you."

"And I love you, too."

He kissed her again.

After a minute, they stepped back from each other, still holding hands.

"I kept my promise," she said.

"You did. I will never forget."

On Christmas Eve, everyone sat in the living room wearing red-and-black pyjamas, Bree had surprised them with.

"Okay, each one of us gets to open a present," Bree announced. She grabbed one for Mark and herself and sat back down on the love seat beside him, waiting.

Rachel found one for Logan and herself and settled back down on the couch.

"Who's going first?" asked Rachel.

"Me," said Bree, giggling and ripping into her box. She soon held up a beautiful dark-blue Ralph Lauren blouse. "Wow. Thank you, Rachel."

"You're welcome. *Direct from Fifth Avenue.*"

Bree continued to admire it. "I love it!"

"My turn," said Mark, who opened his big box. Searching, he finally found a small card inside. He laughed. "Thanks Da!"

"What is it?" asked Rachel.

"A Tim Hortons gift card," answered Mark.

They all chuckled.

Logan faced Rachel. "Your turn."

"This is from Bree and Mark," she said, reading the little tag, as she carefully opened the gift, and laid the wrapping paper down. She examined the contents with a huge smile on her face, finally lifting up a pair of teal sea glass earrings.

"From *Bree's Seaglass*," announced Mark. "We saw you checking them out one day."

Rachel looked at Bree. "Did you make these?"

She nodded her head, smiling. The girls leaned over and embraced.

Rachel turned to Logan. "Your turn."

He opened the large box that sat on the floor in front of him, pulling out his old blue-and-black jacket. "Yay! You're giving it back to me?"

Rachel hopped up and walked over to the entrance area closet and removed a brown leather jacket that hung on a hanger. "Would you like to trade?"

Logan stared at the new coat, which had a zipped up pocket in the left chest area. He whistled. "Wow. I love it." He stood up, as she brought it over. He slid his arms into the jacket, modelling it for all to see.

"Wow stylin' Da!" exclaimed Mark.

"I love it," said Bree.

"Me too," said Logan, as Rachel gave him a big hug.

He gazed at her, "For that, you get to open a gift from me."

"Really?"

He nodded.

She searched through some presents under the tree and found a small flat gift with her name on it. She pulled it out and sat down beside Logan. She shook it. "What could it be?" She unwrapped the paper and opened the box. Peeking inside, she discovered a small bronze key. She pulled it out. "What's this for?"

He grinned. "A mystery key."

She softly punched him in the arm. "Tell me!"

"Sorry, but you'll have to wait until the morning."

"It will drive me crazy."

"I know. Sorry."

She looked at Bree. "Do you know what it's for?"

"Maybe," she said coyly.

"Oh! Mark?"

"Sorry."

"That's it. No mercy from me tonight when we play Hearts."

Everyone laughed, but no one gave away the surprise.

Christmas! Awaking to the smell of pancakes, Rachel climbed out of bed and pushed into her slippers. Still wearing her Christmas pyjamas, she walked down the hallway and strolled into the kitchen. Bree was cooking and the men sat at the table. "Merry Christmas!" Rachel said.

"Merry Christmas!" they shouted in response, with hugs all around. Mark and Bree still had their pyjamas on, but Logan was dressed in his new leather coat over a black sweater and jeans. He looked pretty good, actually.

Rachel sat and looked at the clock. "Wow. Ten after nine. I slept in."

"You must have needed it," said Bree, placing a plate of pancakes in front of her.

Logan slid the butter and maple syrup over to Rachel with a warm smile. "Are you excited?"

"Oh, yeah! Can't wait to find out what that key is for." She took a couple of bites of her pancakes. "These taste great!"

"Thanks," replied Bree.

A short time later, Rachel was finished and the table cleared off. "Let's go open our presents," said Bree. They all headed to their favourite seats in the living room, where Bree dug out gifts for everyone. Most presents were clothing items like Christmas sweaters, toques, mitts, pants, shirts and socks. The usual fare.

Rachel then unwrapped a small box from Bree and Mark. Opening it, she found an elegant sea glass pendant. "Oh, this is lovely. It matches my earrings."

"Glad you like it!" answered Bree.

"I love it!" replied Rachel, getting up and hugging Bree and Mark.

Logan then found another gift for Rachel. "Here ya go," he said.

Sitting back down, she opened the large, flat box. Removing the box top, she discovered a pile of typed pages. The top one read: *Blueberry Kisses* by Logan Stewart.

"Eek!" She placed the box on the coffee table and dove into Logan's arms.

"Don't get too excited. It's only chapter one."

"A new novel?"

"Book two in the *Cape Breton Romance* series."

"Wow. I'm so proud of you, Logan. I can't wait to read it."

"Way to go, Da," said Mark.

"Oh, Da, we're so happy for you," chimed in Bree.

Rachel sat patiently while everyone opened the remaining gifts, which were mostly clothing items.

"Well, that's it," said Bree. "Who wants a coffee or tea?"

"Looks like there's one more," Rachel said, pointing to an envelope laying between two branches part way up the tree, which Bree had missed — not knowing it had been placed there early in the morning.

Bree rose and examined it. "What's this?"

"Just a little gift for you and Mark."

Bree picked it up and brought it over to Mark. She sat on the armrest. "Do you want to open it?" she asked him.

"No, you go ahead."

Bree opened it carefully and pulled out a cheque for $5,000. She and Mark stared at each other and then faced Rachel. "Um, Rachel?"

Rachel reached for Logan's hand. "I spoke with Logan before I wrote it, but I wanted to help you with your back taxes and having a great start for the new year."

Bree handed the cheque to Mark. All eyes were on him.

"We can't take this," he finally said.

"Why not?" Rachel replied.

"Because, well, it's too much."

Rachel leaned forward. "Mark, and Bree, please

listen to me. I knew you would have trouble accepting this, but I feel like we have become so close, like family."

"We feel the same," said Bree.

"Yes, and I have done well for many years, and I have the funds. They're just sitting in a bank collecting interest. I want to help you. It's actually a blessing for me. After all, *it's more blessed to give than receive*, right?"

Bree and Mark gazed at each other until Mark finally broke into a smile that became a grin. "Alright then. What do you say, Bree?"

Bree jumped up. "Yes! Thank you, Rachel!"

Rachel met the couple in the middle of the room, where they embraced! Logan quickly joined them.

"Thank you so much," said Mark. "This really takes the pressure off."

Bree turned to him. "Maybe now you won't have to go out west in the spring."

He kissed her. "Yeah, maybe I won't have to!"

Later that morning, Logan faced Rachel. "Are you ready to find out what the key opens?"

"Eek! Yes!"

"Let's go, then."

"Are you guys coming?" she asked Bree and Mark.

"Nope," they replied in unison, both grinning.

Logan faced Mark. "I need your keys."

Mark dug them out of his pocket and threw them to

his dad.

Logan gazed at Rachel. "The truck is getting fixed. Should have it back in a week or so."

"Good." She loved that truck and wanted it back asap.

Shortly thereafter, Rachel sat beside Logan in the Toyota, passing through Whitney Pier and Sydney. Soon, they drove down Charlotte Street, the shopping district that she loved. She turned to Logan. "What have you been up to?"

He grinned. "Oh, nothing." He pulled over. "Let's see if that key fits any of these doors. Did you bring it?"

Digging into a pocket of her black leather jacket, she held it up. "Are you kidding me?"

"Let's go!" he said.

She fluttered her eyelashes. "Before we go, got any more of those blueberry kisses?"

"As many as you want." They leaned over and kissed.

She smiled. "Yummy. I want a lot."

"Me too."

They got out and walked hand-in-hand a few blocks down one side of the street. There was still lots of snow around, but the sidewalks had been cleared. She looked up. The sun was bright and warm on this blue-sky day. She chuckled to herself, as she thought of them holding hands and wearing leather jackets. They were like twenty-somethings. She snapped out of her thoughts and searched for doors to try. Logan teased her often, asking her if the key might belong to this shop or that one.

"Let's cross the street and try the other side," he suggested.

They walked for a few minutes more, her eyes darting ahead to each building, trying to figure out which door to try. As they walked past a ladies clothing store, which sidetracked her for a moment, she saw it! A shop window ahead with gold lettering:

RACHEL ABRAMS
Literary Agent
Submissions welcome

"Eek! Logan! What have you done!"

"Merry Christmas and Happy Hanukkah!" he exclaimed. They embraced.

"Merry Christmas!"

"Check it out."

She walked over to the window and peered in. The building was empty, except for a counter in the middle with a telephone sitting upon it.

"I thought I would leave the decorating to you. That is, if you like the idea. You don't have to."

"I love it!" She felt like a kid at five in the morning on Christmas day, opening the gift they wanted so bad.

"Try the key."

She walked into the narrow entrance area and stuck the key in. "Turn it with me," she said.

He reached around her and they both turned it

together. *Click*. She pushed the door open and they walked in. It smelled of fresh paint and was about fifteen feet wide and forty feet in length. The walls were white and the floor made of blue tiles.

"Let's leave the door open so it airs out," said Logan.

"Good idea." She noticed a note pad and pen by the phone. "You think of everything, don't you?"

"I try, ma'am."

There was a doorway in the back of the space, so Rachel strolled over to it and peeked inside. "Ah, a little office. Perfect!"

Logan leaned on the counter. "I thought this could be a start for you. You can change anything you want. Bring in any furniture. Change any words or lettering on the window."

She hugged him again. "I love it, Logan. I have thought about this so often. It's the perfect start. The perfect gift."

Logan gazed at her. "Bree has been working on your new website."

"Are you kidding me? A website already?"

"Yup, and Mark is checking on advertising, and planning a grand opening."

She took a step back and gazed up at him, still holding his hands. "I feel like God has given me a bigger gift this year, Logan. Bigger than all of my gifts and this new office, which is the best Christmas present ever. *Family*."

He smiled. "We feel the same. You're a part of our

family now, and always will be."

At that moment, a young woman with long brown hair walked into the office, followed by a middle-aged man. She smiled. "Are you open?"

Rachel chuckled. "No, sorry. This is actually my Christmas present."

"Oh, sorry. We were driving by, on the way to my Grandma's, when I saw the sign in your window."

"Are you an author?" asked Rachel.

"She's been writing stories since she was a kid," said the man, who Rachel assumed to be her father. "All her friends and family think she should be published."

Rachel glanced at Logan and addressed the aspiring writer. "Have you already looked for an agent?"

"Oh, yes. Some even asked for a full manuscript, but there's always a reason they don't like it in the end."

Rachel raised her eyebrows. "The fact that they asked for a full manuscript is a feather in your cap."

A huge grin spread across the young woman's face. "Really?"

"Yes. What's your name?"

"Amy Jones. This is my dad, Tanner."

Rachel stuck out her hand. "Pleased to meet you, Amy and Tanner. I'm Rachel Abrams and this is Logan."

Logan shook hands with the visitors.

Rachel turned to Logan. "Do we have an email?"

"Hmm. I don't know. Maybe call Bree."

Rachel dug out her phone. "Hi Bree. Do we have an

email address? I have someone at my new office who needs to send us her manuscript ... Yes, that's right."

Logan grabbed the paper and pen.

"Rachel Abrams at hot mail dot com. Thanks, Bree. And, yes, I love the new office! Talk soon."

Logan wrote it down.

Rachel folded the paper and handed it to Amy. "Send me the first three chapters of your latest novel in a PDF. How about that?"

Amy twirled. "That would be fantastic!" she said, putting the paper into her purse. "You have made my day! Merry Christmas!"

"Merry Christmas," returned Rachel, as everyone wished each other the same. Amy and her dad left, got into their truck and drove off, waving to Rachel and Logan.

"That was amazing," said Logan.

"Yes, it was. She reminds me of myself, many years ago." She reached out and took Logan's hand. "I can't wait to see what she's written. This is what got me excited when I first entered the business. How thrilling to be a young author and waiting to see what an agent thinks of your work."

"Or, even an *older* author."

"Yes, even an older author." She snuggled up to him, her head resting against his chest. "Thank you for this gift, Logan."

He kissed the top of her head.

12

One Year Later

Rachel felt like a whale. It was the afternoon on Christmas Day, and they'd just gobbled down a delicious turkey meal that Mark had prepared. The big bird had come with stuffing, cranberry sauce, potatoes, turnip and carrots. Afterwards, in the living room, Bree served tea and coffee with blueberry pie. As they all relaxed, Rachel thought back to the morning, when Logan had opened the special gift she'd gotten him.

"Let's open our gifts!" exclaimed Bree, sitting on the armrest beside Mark.

"Who goes first?" asked Logan, sitting beside Rachel on the couch.

"Rachel!" replied Bree.

Rachel got up, found a present and sat back down. She opened it. It was a red Christmas sweater with snowmen, from Bree and Mark. She held it up. "It's wonderful. I love it!"

"You're next, Da," said Mark.

He stood, looked under the tree, and dug out a small gift. "This is from you," he said to Rachel, sitting back down.

She beamed, hoping he'd like it.

He unwrapped it. "Wow. Are you kidding me?" He held up a gold bracelet with a thick bar.

"Wow," said Mark and Bree together.

"Read the inscription," said Rachel.

"*Promise Me Forever*," replied Logan. "Sweet." He held out his arm and Rachel clasped it on. They kissed and she snuggled beside him.

"Your turn, Bree," said Rachel.

"Instead of opening a gift, we have an announcement," she replied, grinning and wrapping an arm around Mark. "We're expecting."

"Oh my goodness!" shouted Rachel, jumping up and rushing over to the couple.

Logan was on her heels, embracing everyone. "Congratulations! I can't believe it! You two will make great parents." He gazed at Rachel. "We're going to have a grandchild."

Rachel smiled. "Next Christmas is going to be extra special."

"Let's celebrate with hot chocolate," said Bree. She went to the kitchen and brought back the hot drinks a short time later.

Sipping her drink, Rachel mused on the past year. And what a year it had been. Besides the office in Sydney, she now owned a small publishing firm, Cove

Island Press, with Lena in Connecticut. Logan became their first official signing. Soon after, they offered Amy Jones a contract and she and her family were over the moon. The young author was incredibly gifted and wrote wonderful cozy mysteries.

Rachel had then hired Bree and Mark as official part-time employees, which, together with their cruise ship business, meant that Mark could stay home. Bree thanked her often for the gift last year and the new jobs. And the jobs were not charity, either, as Rachel's new staff were worth their weight in gold. Bree was the first set of eyes on new submissions, and edited manuscripts they liked. Mark did all kinds of local, low cost promotions and handled their social media, which really helped to spread the word. It turned out that Cape Breton was a gold mine of storytellers just waiting to be discovered.

Rachel was now splitting her time between Connecticut and the Cape, and enjoyed every minute of her new life. Lena ran the US office perfectly and they also hired a small staff. They received many excellent submissions and picked a few winners. The giant bookstore chains were in constant contact with Lena and Zach. With Lena nudging him along, he had resigned from Big Apple and become their new head of Sales and Marketing.

After Zach joined the new firm, he informed Rachel and Lena that things were falling apart at Big Apple. They'd lost most of their top executives, and Nick and his new staff were having trouble finding new books and authors. In fact, a few of their established authors contacted Cove Island Press about novels they were currently writing.

Big Apple meetings deteriorated often into shouting matches, and the general consensus was that Mel had no clue what she was doing. Rachel took no real joy in the destruction of Big Apple, but it did give her some satisfaction. Regardless, she was moving on.

She often thought back on her first two cruises to Cape Breton to when she'd first met Mark, Bree and Logan. She had no idea her life was going to change so dramatically. At first, she had trepidation about all the big changes, but later learned to embrace them. Logan imparted a lot of wisdom to her and was a great help in navigating new waters. He'd even visited Connecticut a couple of times. He loved it and never pressured her to move permanently to Canada. She showed him the new office, introducing him to everyone, and brought him to her favourite spots — West Beach and Cove Island.

As she thought about summer and beaches, she remembered back to August, when Logan had taken her to Dominion Beach, a short drive from South Bar. They'd walked along the sandy shore, hand-in-hand. She loved the popular spot, but it was crowded on warm days. After school began, he took her there again, on a Thursday in early September. They had the beach all to themselves. They spent half the day there, sitting on a blanket facing the sea, eating a nice lunch they'd packed and taking long strolls along the water's edge. She asked him to include the spot in his latest novel.

In late summer, they'd also picked tons of blueberries in Low Point. Lots of the little berries never made it into Brees baking, though, as Rachel ate handfuls out of her bucket as they picked. She smiled, remembering how Logan caught her eating them. He'd become her best friend and rock and she couldn't be more in love.

Taking another sip of hot chocolate, she noticed Logan gazing at her.

"How about a nice drive?" he asked.

"Sounds lovely. It's so beautiful out. Where to?"

"You'll see."

A half hour later, they turned down Brown's Road towards the lighthouse.

Rachel smiled. "Ah, good choice. Haven't been here since the summer."

"Yeah."

They parked, got out and walked around the lighthouse. Standing on the snow-covered ground, they faced the ocean. It was chilly, with light fog rolling in.

She turned to face him. "This always reminds me of *Promise Me Forever*. I think I started to fall in love with you after I read that last chapter."

"And I'm so glad you did ... *Oh my goodness*." He pointed behind her. "Why is there a cruise ship in today?"

She spun, but saw nothing but fog and the grey sea. She turned back towards Logan, who was kneeling and holding a small white box with a red ribbon.

"*Logan*," she whispered. She took the box and opened it. Lifting the elegant ring, she examined it — a spectacular diamond on a gold band. "It's *so* beautiful."

"Rachel Abrams, will you—

"Yes!" She jumped into his arms, causing them to tumble into the snow. They kissed and then just lay on their backs, laughing.

"Don't lose the ring!" he shouted.

"Never!" she answered. They got up and Rachel handed him the box. She removed her glove, extending her arm and hand.

Logan pushed the engagement ring onto her finger. It fit perfectly.

She admired it, then gazed at him.

Gazing deep into her eyes, he wrapped his strong arms around her, grabbing the back of her coat and pulled her into a tight embrace. "You've made me the happiest man alive."

"And I'm the happiest woman."

Logan whispered in her ear: "*He gazed deep into her eyes and knew it was true. He grabbed her and they kissed again. Long and deep. They stayed in each other's arms for what seemed like forever. He had won her heart. And that was all that mattered.*"

Rachel sighed and leaned her head back. Their lips met. A minute later, she licked her lips. "You taste like ..."

He laughed. "Blueberries?"

She giggled. "No, hot chocolate."

He kissed her again.

Driving back to Mark and Bree's, Rachel debated to bring up something that was troubling her. She didn't want to wreck the wonderful moment and day, but it was intimately connected. She stared down at her sparkling ring. She totally loved it. "Logan?"

"Yes."

"Did you see the large white house for sale close to Mark and Bree's?"

"Yeah, it went on sale in November. I heard the family wants to stay out west."

"I checked it out online."

Logan glanced at her. "You don't want to live on the top of White's Lane?"

"Please don't be offended. I wanted to bring this up before, but didn't want to hurt your feelings."

"There's nothing you can't discuss with me."

She gazed out the front window. "It's kind of isolated up there. And, in winter the plows have a hard time driving to the top. And then there was the coyote attack. I still think I have PTSD from that — and it happened to you and Mark. I don't think I'm ready to live in the woods, just yet.

"I'm still a city girl at heart. Actually, I'm somewhere in between. In between the girl I was in Montana and the woman I became in New York."

He reached over and held her hand.

She turned to him. "Do you understand what I'm trying to say?"

He glanced at her. "I think so. You've had a lot of big changes in the past year, plus you're a social person, who needs people and interaction. You don't want to be stuck in a small house in the middle of nowhere."

"Yes. That's it in a nutshell." She unbuckled herself and slid next to him. Buckling herself in again, she held his hand between hers. "I want to spend the rest of my life with you."

"Well that's good, we just got engaged."

She laughed. "Could we look at the house?"

"Absolutely. I just want you to be comfortable."

Rachel was relieved. That was the only stumbling block she saw in their future together. The way Logan handled it gave her great confidence in their relationship. He could have gotten mad or upset, but didn't. This was the kind of man she needed in her life. She flashed back to volatile Nick in the restaurant that night and was glad she'd escaped that trap. *Poor Melanie.*

They closed in on South Bar. "Now, where is that place?" asked Logan.

"I think it's three or four houses past Bree's."

Logan slowed down. "There it is. They drove down

168

the long driveway and parked right beside the *For Sale* sign."

"It's a two-level split," Rachel said.

He faced her. "Call the number."

Her eyebrows arched. "Really?"

"Yeah, but it will probably just go to an answering machine."

Rachel phoned and got prepared to leave a message, when suddenly a man answered. "Oh, hi, Merry Christmas," she greeted. "Sorry to bother you during the holidays, but my boyf ... my *fiance* and I are parked outside a property in South Bar. What? Really? Yes, we'll be right here." She hung up and gazed at Logan.

"He's coming?"

She nodded. "Yes. He said he lives in Whitney Pier and is popping over right now."

Logan smiled. "Well, let's get out and look around."

They climbed out and trudged through the snow, taking in the house and neighbourhood. Walking into the tree-lined backyard, they could almost touch the ocean.

"The yard is similar to Mark's," said Logan.

"And a big deck, too. Summers would be wonderful."

Logan pointed. "I think I can see Mark's deck from here."

She swayed from side to side. "We'd be neighbours. Wouldn't that be wonderful?"

He put an arm around her. "Sure would."

A few minutes later, they heard a vehicle approaching

and met the realtor around front.

The short man climbed out of his truck and walked up to them, hand extended. "Hello, I'm John Peterson." They all shook hands.

"Nice to meet you," said Logan and Rachel in unison.

He gestured towards the house. "Well, let's have a look inside." He unlocked the front door and they strolled in, removing their boots. Stairs rose and descended from the entrance area. Climbing the steps, they stood in the furnished living room. The layout was remarkably similar to Bree's, including the all-important fireplace. Rachel pointed to it and smiled, as they followed the real estate agent around. Logan nodded.

Walking into the kitchen, Rachel noticed that the colours and appliances were rather drab, but she didn't care. She wanted to put her own stamp on the place anyway, if they decided to get it. Sliding glass doors led to the deck. She stood there, staring out at the ocean. It had become so important to her. It was spiritual. It connected her to Connecticut, the lighthouse, the past, the present, everything.

They took a quick tour of the bedrooms and the downstairs. Everything seemed to be in great shape. They returned to the living room upstairs, where Rachel and Logan gazed out the main window. "I love it," she whispered to Logan.

He squeezed her hand in support.

They turned to face the agent.

"The family is looking for a quick sale," the realtor said. "They're going to get a ton of offers as soon as the holidays are over."

Rachel glanced at Logan and then spoke to the agent. "What are the options for a down payment and mortgage payments?"

He looked at his papers. "Let's see. If you could put, say, forty thousand down, it would leave you with payments of fourteen hundred monthly."

Logan raised his eyebrows and whistled. "What shape is the furnace and electrical in?"

"New furnace, hot water tank, wiring. Everything is up to code. The family lived here for a month, but the husband got a big offer in Edmonton and had to return right away."

Rachel smiled. "Can we be alone for a minute?"

"Of course. I'll wait in my truck. Take your time."

"Thank you," said Logan, as the man left.

She grabbed Logan's hand. "Oh, Logan, I want this house so badly. I love the location, the proximity to the ocean, and we'd be right beside Mark and Bree."

"It's a lot of money."

"If we don't snap it up, it'll be gone soon."

"Yeah, I suppose so."

"I've got the funds," she said.

He raised his eyebrows again. "Are you sure?"

"Yes."

"Well, you could put in an offer."

"Really? You don't think I'm crazy?"

"Yeah, a little, but who isn't? Life is a risk."

She laughed.

He gazed deep into her eyes. "And I'll sell the house in Low Point. We could get the monthly payments down."

"Oh my goodness! You'd do that for me? Are you sure?"

"Of course. One hundred and ten percent."

"Oh, Logan, I couldn't be happier!" She jumped into his arms and pulled his head down, her lips pressing into his. After a minute, she leaned her head back. "I love you forever."

"Promise?"

She kissed him again.

After speaking to the very happy agent, they immediately drove to Mark and Bree's to share the incredible news.

"We're back," announced Logan, as they walked in.

Rachel put a finger to her lips. "Let's surprise them."

"C'mon in," shouted Bree. "I'm making hot chocolate."

They sat on the couch as Bree served. She returned and settled in Mark's chair.

"How was the lighthouse?" Mark asked, entering the living room and sitting on the armrest.

"Eek!" An ear-splitting shriek jolted everyone as Bree jumped up.

"What the?" questioned Mark.

"Congratulations!" shouted Bree, barely containing herself as Rachel rose to hug her.

"What is it?" asked Mark again, getting to his feet.

"Show him!" shouted Bree.

Rachel extended her hand, as Mark's mouth fell open. He hugged her tight, as Logan stood.

"Da!" exclaimed Mark, as he shook his father's hand and embraced him.

Bree gave Logan a bear hug also.

"Before you sit down, we have more exciting news," said Rachel.

Mark and Bree's eyes got big. "*More news*?" asked Bree.

"Don't worry, I'm not pregnant."

They all laughed.

"We might be buying a new house," Rachel blurted.

"Eek!" Bree screamed again.

"We might be neighbours," Logan said.

"That house," replied Mark, pointing in the right direction.

Logan nodded. "Yup."

"Oh my goodness," squealed Bree, as they all hugged again.

A minute later, Bree looked at her husband. "Mark, come and help me." They left for the kitchen.

Rachel and Logan settled back on the couch.

"I feel exhausted," said Rachel, snuggling up to her love.

He wrapped his arm around her. "Me too."

She held up her hand and let the afternoon sun sparkle off her diamond. She admired it for some time. "I don't think I've ever been happier in my life ... *Ever.*"

ACKNOWLEDGEMENTS

I would like to thank:

Silke
for editing, graphic artwork, and typesetting

Nora Campbell & Mitzi Hathway
for their encouragement and support

Early Readers:
Leslie Ann MacIsaac, Pearl Egdell,
Priscille Belliveau, Susan Odo,
Darlene Desveaux, Alice Quigley

Proofreaders:
Jill Corley & Maria Ayala

Thank you for reading!

Please leave a rating and/or comment
at Amazon.ca or Amazon.com

For more information about
our books, please visit
randalljamesbooks.com

Turn the page to read
the first chapter of local bestseller
Cape Breton Orphan

A story of survival, overcoming, and hope

CAPE BRETON ORPHAN

a memoir

WITH BONUS
SHORT STORY
'The Hockey
Gloves'

RANDALL JAMES

1

Launch

In 1969, Apollo 11 landed on the moon, and in 1969, I met my mother. I was eight years old.

That summer, the Red Barn, a fast-food restaurant in London, Ontario, the town I lived in, held an Apollo 11 contest. You had to collect colourful stickers showing the spacecraft at different points of the mission and sticker them in a large cardboard folder. I vividly remember the photo of the splashdown, the large red-and-white striped parachutes open and the re-entry pod landing in the water.

Customers of the Red Barn received stickers with their purchases, but I think the manager gave me a few each day, even when I didn't buy anything.

I filled all the blank rectangles in the folder over time, and then put it in the draw box. A week later, we received a phone call. I had won! The prize was a meal at the Red Barn for myself, my dad, and my mother. My sister Alison, one and a half years older than I, was able to substitute, which was great, because we didn't have a mother, and nobody wanted to leave out Alison anyway.

When we went for our free meal, we found out that I had also won a toy: a cool battery-powered robot. It moved around on our table as we enjoyed ourselves and had a great family time.

Which wasn't all that normal because Dad popped in and out of our lives.

He was in the airborne I believe, as I remember photos of him jumping out of aircraft. But that only partly accounts for the shaky existence Alison and I were used to. We moved around a lot, living at different houses and with different people — mostly without our father.

Just like orphans.

I have memories of being with various families through those early years in London. One family took us to a church service. The same people, coming back from a short vacation, gave me a toy western gun and holster set, the belt containing bullets.

Once, there was a flood and we swam in the streets. I distinctly remember this, but sometimes wonder if it was a dream.

Alison and I also lived with the Blairs, an older couple who fixed and sold bicycles. They taught me to ride a bike. We spent the most time with the Blairs out of all the families who looked after us. Their house was close to the Red Barn restaurant.

My dad had a place too, on Dundas Street, a rented room in a building inhabited by people we didn't know, and we stayed there with him when he was in town.

Dad dated various women through the years. One night, very late, Alison and I woke up from some noise. Dad had a woman over and they were in his bed. We were all sleeping in the one room. I think the woman was French. She made us warm milk, and I drifted off to sleep again after drinking it.

Once, my father showed up after a longer absence with a new full beard, almost unrecognizable, and it scared me.

Two incidents happened during those years that make me wonder today about his mental state.

He had a red VW Bug (with Alison's and my baby shoes dangling from the review mirror). One evening, he took us kids to a drive-in movie with his date. We lay in the back and fell asleep. I awoke during a horror movie and watched a woman in a wedding dress turn into a skeleton. I was so frightened! (It's possible Dad had woken us up to see it.)

Another time, Alison and I were fetched from our beds in the middle of the night and brought down to the basement. My father and his friends had stolen turkeys and were killing them right there and then. The birds ran around in a frenzy, some with their heads cut off. It was loud, bizarre and scary.

Did my dad and his friends do drugs? Sometimes I wonder. I think my dad had grown up as an orphan as well. That would explain a lot.

But Dad did something nice for me once: he saved my life. I was popping PEZ dispenser candies into my mouth, when the spring and plastic top came out and flew into my throat. I was choking.

There was panic in the house and no one knew what to do. Suddenly, my dad walked in the front door, looked at me and shoved his hand down my throat and pulled the thing out. Wow. It was amazing.

In 1966, Alison and my dad took me to my first day of school. They brought me to the entrance, but I had to go in all by myself.

When I was in second grade, Boyle Memorial Elementary School sent a note to my father, proposing for me to skip Grade 3, but he would not allow it. Looking back, I think it was a good decision.

By that point, we lived close to the Kellogg's (Corn Flakes) plant. Also nearby was Queen's Park. We went there with my father, only a couple of days before my mother came for us. I can remember a few last things with Dad shortly before leaving: having French fries at a restaurant and climbing with him on Engine 86, the old train that stood in the park. Dad knew what was about to happen, but he didn't tell us anything.

One day in the summer, a pretty woman with long dark hair and green eyes showed up at my dad's house.

It was my mother.

She arrived together with a man named Johnny in a black car. I remember meeting her, and going with her to the trunk of the car. She had two new turtle-neck shirts for me: one yellow, the other purple. Both had a large silver ring at the top of the zipper and looked spacey. I put on the yellow one right away.

A short time later, on the same day, my sister and I sat in the back seat of the Impala and drove away with Johnny McPhee and Ma.

So, where had she been all that time?

Years later, I found out. My mother, Deanna, became pregnant at a young age, and was forced to leave her home in New Waterford, Cape Breton, and stay with relatives (the Hubbards) in London, Ontario. There she met my dad, Bob, a friend of the Hubbards. They married shortly after and had three children in quick succession. Bradley was born in January 1959, Alison in December of the same year, and I in May 1961. Ma was nineteen when she gave birth to me.

I have seen a couple of black-and-white photographs of us three kids sitting on the floor together, myself a baby at the time. My mother must have left shortly after, taking only Bradley with her, as she returned to Cape Breton.

Ma told me years later about a train ride from Ontario to Nova Scotia when I was about three. She must have gotten Alison and me for a visit to Cape Breton. While playing in the compartment, I cut my forehead on an ashtray that jutted out from the wall. The accident happened in New Brunswick. They tried to stem the bleeding with a lot of towels, but couldn't, and finally had to stop the train to get medical help. The injury left a small scar at the top of my forehead.

I can't recall any other details of that trip, and I don't know why my mother didn't keep my sister and me then.

But here she finally was, taking us away.

I don't remember saying good-bye to dad, or any tears. Nothing.

The black Impala rolled out of his driveway. I felt neither joyful to be with my mother nor sad about leaving my father, or London. I went along with it all. I think I was extremely internal at the time.

The first night of our trip we stayed at a private house in Belleville, Ontario. The owners must have been connected to hockey great Bobby Hull, because they had a signed hockey stick and a big poster of him hanging on the wall. Once in a while, I wonder who it was, because Hull is from the area.

The next day, we got stuck in a major traffic jam in Quebec for a couple of hours. A Quebecois man, the driver of a car in front, brought Johnny a newspaper. It was in French, though, which none of us could understand, but it was still a nice gesture.

We had a long drive, but I don't remember any other particulars.

Did I even know we were on the way to Cape Breton? Did I even understand any of it? I don't think so.

I was on autopilot.

Turn the page to read
Chapter 1 of
Blueberry Kisses
the sequel to
Promise Me Forever
by Randall James

Blueberry Kisses

Rachel strolled along the sandy shore of Dominion Beach. It was a perfectly warm and sunny afternoon, with a light breeze from the ocean washing over her. Dressed in jean cut-offs and a white summer blouse, open over a tee, she stopped to examine a sea shell. Lifting it to her ear, she listened to the sound of the ocean. She chuckled and tossed it into the sea, continuing to walk.

She loved the feel of the cool, wet sand on the bottom of her feet and between her toes. Turning around, she saw Logan, wearing only long shorts, running towards her. She laughed and jogged ahead — her hair flowing behind. She glanced over her shoulder. He was gaining on her. She giggled and kept running.

"Hey, wait up," he hollered.

She laughed and kept running.

"Rachel," he hollered.

She chuckled.

"Rachel!" she heard again, but the voice wasn't Logan's.

Looking over her shoulder, she saw Nick, dressed in a business suit and racing towards her. Fear gripped her as she ran faster.

"Rachel!" he shouted again, angrily.

Picking up the pace, she glanced back. He gained on her.

"Get away from me!" she shouted.

Her heart pounding, Rachel awoke and sat up. Sweat poured from her forehead.

Logan's eyes opened. "Are you okay?"

"I had a bad dream." She reached for him, laying her head on his chest.

"I thought I heard you mumbling," he said sleepily, hugging her.

"It was just a dream," she said, not wanting to tell him it was about Nick.

Logan softly stroked her hair. "It was just a dream," he repeated.

It was just a dream, she told herself over and over, as she listened to his steady heart-beat. After a while, she drifted off.

"Whoa, Da!"

Logan's line pulled tight. A big mackerel fought him hard. He smiled. He and Mark hadn't gone fishing together since last summer. They'd waved good-bye to the girls this sunny morning, and pushed the little boat out into the water, just behind Mark's house. They drifted for a while towards Low Point and got a few nibbles right away.

Grinning, Logan thought about Rachel as he reeled in the fish. She was going to love the mackerel. The ladies had gone shopping in Sydney.

Mark pulled the line into the boat. "You got three beauties, Da! I want to eat some of our catch tonight."

"Yeah, sounds good." Logan sat back and looked around — surprised to see that they were just off the Low Point lighthouse. It instantly brought back a thousand memories to him — his biggest one, getting engaged. He smiled, as a soft breeze blew through his hair.

Mark turned to face him. "I think we have our limit, Da. Should we head back?"

"Yup. Can't wait till the girls see what we caught."

Rachel, wearing a sleeveless white shirt and blue jeans, and Bree sporting a pink maternity top, strolled down a busy Charlotte Street on the glistering June day. It was just past noon. The ladies were giddy and carefree, stopping in various shops to browse clothes for themselves and the baby. Bree was in fantastic shape for being seven months pregnant. The baby clothes they were searching for were pink. Mark and Bree had found that out in February.

Logan was over the moon. Rachel smiled when she recalled how Logan reacted when they had told them after supper one night. "We're going to have a granddaughter," he repeated over and over, beaming at Rachel.

Mark and Bree had wasted no time in getting the baby room ready, changing everything in the room that Rachel used to sleep in. Bree had shown her one morning when she'd popped over for coffee. They already had a crib, mobile, dresser, baby change table, and a bassinet for when the baby would come home from the hospital. The bottom half of the room had been painted pink and the top stayed white.

Rachel was admiring a light-blue blouse in the latest store, when Bree strolled over to her. "Do you like it?"

"Yeah, love it."

"Try it on."

Rachel did and came out modelling in front of the mirror.

"*You look fabulous, darling*," Bree said.

Rachel laughed.

Bree gazed at her. "Can I get it for you?"

"No, I'll get it," replied Rachel, walking back to the change room and taking it off.

"Can I see it?" asked Bree, as Rachel came out and walked up to her.

Rachel handed it to her and Bree immediately took off for the cash register.

"Hey," hollered Rachel.

"You pay for everything," Bree yelled over her shoulder. "I'm getting this."

Rachel laughed and gave up. It was true — she was always paying for everything. She had to remember to let others pay sometimes.

Bree handed her the bag as they walked outside. "Here ya go, sister."

"Why, thanks, Deary." Rachel's arms were getting tired from carrying so many bags. "Should we put the bags in the car and go for lunch?"

Bree smiled. "Sounds great. I'm starving." She swung the bags on one arm. "I think Missy has enough clothes for two years now."

Rachel chuckled. "What time do we need to be back?"

"The boys will be back from fishing around two, I think Mark said."

"Good, we have about an hour and a half."

Bree's car was parked by the boardwalk. They stood at the cross-walk and waited for the light to change. As they chatted while crossing, Rachel caught a speeding car out of the corner of her eye. The dark car accelerated down Charlotte Street towards them. Bree hadn't noticed.

"Watch out! Rachel screamed, as she pushed Bree towards the sidewalk — and safety.

"*What the hell*?!" Bree yelled, falling towards the curb.

At that moment, a red Audi pulled out from the side of the road. The speeding car smashed into the side of it, causing the red car to catapult towards Rachel. She tried to jump out of the way, but it was too late.

Rachel had a brief feeling of flying through the air before blacking out. When she came to, some minutes later, Bree was kneeling beside her with tears in her eyes.

"It's okay," said Bree, brushing Rachel's forehead softly. "I'm here. An ambulance is on the way."

Rachel didn't know why. She smiled at Bree and looked up at the bright blue sky. "Nick," she said to Bree.

Bree leaned closer to her. "What?"

"Nick."

"What about Nick?"

Rachel heard sirens getting louder and felt tired. She gazed at beautiful Bree.

Tears rolled down Brees cheeks. "Hang in there, Rachel. I'm with you. *Please God help us. Please help Rachel.*"

Rachel thought it was sweet that Bree was praying for her. God was nice. He would help them. She smiled and looked back up at the sky. It was so blue ...

Other Books by Randall James

Youth & Family

Jace Power & the Battle of Mars City

Jace Power & the Rebels of Jupiter

Gold & Sharpe

Tyler Hicks & the Battle of Alpha Centauri

The Strikerz

Memoirs

Cape Breton Orphan

Cape Breton Orphan Returns

For more information about
Randall James
and his books, please visit:

randalljamesbooks.com

Randall James grew up on spectacular Cape Breton Island, NS, and now resides on beautiful Vancouver Island, BC. He likes to walk along the shore in the day and gaze at stars at night.